Kate Adams, a
slight problem:
pretty vital, so ...
super delirious?

..., a ghost, or just

A quirky guy greets her, explains that she's been in an accident and is now a spirit traveler. What? He offers her a cup of tea, and the drink calms her just enough to follow her annoying spirit guide around. And then, as if things couldn't get any worse, the Hotel Hereafter is booked and she's bunking with a handsome but arrogant Englishman Richard Bennett in the only cottage left for spirit travelers. Once Kate and Richard's angst toward one another clears, it's all coming up roses. But one major complication remains—they return to their mortal lives with no recollection of their ghostly rendezvous.

Six months after the accident, while visiting her former dance teacher in England, Kate runs into Richard. Their touch releases a shared jolt of déjà vu of their romantic stay in the Hereafter. Drawn together and a little panicked by this mysterious connection, Richard pursues the woman he is certain he loves from another place in time. Resistant at first, Kate struggles to come to terms with what she's learned. Lingering dreams that bind her to him give her the extra boost. When Kate confronts Richard's brother, Will, about his secretive role in one of her visions, Will's reaction to the threat he perceives from her renders Kate a criminal target. And it's up to her to outsmart the man who wants her to disappear or she might not have the chance to dance the lead with Richard—because she'll be dead.

Another Place in Time
Copyright 2020 by Anna Fox
ISBN: 978-1-68361-456-2

Cover art by Fantasia Frog Designs

Published by Decadent Publishing Company, LLC
Look for us online at:
www.decadentpublishing.com

Thank you for reading my book! It means so much to me to finally have it out for the world to see. Getting it written was no easy feat. I wrote the first draft in a closet on my laptop using an ironing board! My twins were 3 and my oldest 8 so that was where I went to find solitude. I could not get the idea of Richard and Kate falling in love out of their bodies from my mind so I did whatever it took. It wasn't easy but I loved the story and kept pressing forward, late nights and all, to explore the what-ifs and unknowns. It has been an amazing experience to delve into the issue of life after death. And to see what the writing muse downloaded in to my brain when I sat to write my first novel was always an adventure. The Hereafter is the place I hope will be seen as the mystery of what's to come...ooh cool name for another book!

I would love to hear from you. You can reach me at anna@annafoxauthor.com

Happy Reading!

A. Fox

Another Place in Time

By
Anna Fox

Somewhere in time a place exists so rare the night shines blue,
A place reality echoes and dreams whisper true.
The senses are more heightened and the spirit soars aware,
The impossible exists here and the travelers unaware.

Chapter One
Spirit Travel

Kate Adams was sure about one thing—she did not remember dying.

Perfect eyesight always held her life in clear focus, but she needed an eye exam ASAP. Why? Because standing in a kaleidoscope tunnel had her vision spinning. Stray pieces of dark hair fell loose around her face, and the tight bun she styled earlier now drooped down her head like gelato melting down a sugar cone.

The forced vibrato of a man clearing his throat jolted her. When an elfin man in an oversized silver suit showed up out of nowhere, her jaw dropped.

"I'm Nick. You have vacated your body. Welcome to your spirit travel."

I'm a ghost?

She fumbled for the walls to find something to grip; ethereal clouds formed around her and through the tunnel, creating no solid surface to brace herself against.

"Sorry to keep you waiting." Nick yawned. "You weren't supposed to be alone. Busy night. Hands inside at all times, don't want to get sucked into another dimension. Much harder to get you to the Hotel Hereafter."

Yeah right. There had to be a hidden camera, but where? She had to hand it to the guy. His acting skills were out of this world.

Didn't Nick being an Oscar winning actor with unique dialogue seem the only explanation? She crinkled her nose at him when he juggled paperwork then put it under his arm.

The tunnel stopped spinning, and the clouds cleared to expose flecks of mirrored glass. When she eyed her reflection, disbelief stared back. Her long dark hair, usually smooth and styled, resembled a snarled free-for-all, and her green eyes glowed like radioactive stones. She gulped at the haunting image staring back at her. The pumpkin-colored prom dress from Bo Peep's collection had her first in line for a serious makeover.

Most lucid nightmare ever. It had to be the only explanation for the shocking ensemble she wore. The first thing to put on her shopping list when she woke up had to be a dream catcher.

Adding to the bombardment of unsettling questions, why did she have no memory of how she got to the time warp movie set? Nick mumbled about The Hotel Hereafter, spirit-traveling jet lag, and not being in her body for a while.

I've been drugged! She wrapped her arms around her waist, hugging herself in an attempt to remain cool. Not to mention, the breeze had picked up and the wave of swirling lights mingled with the smell of burnt marshmallows made her queasy. Beyond time for answers, she had frowned at Nick long enough. Her parched mouth creaked open.

"Who put you up to this?" She stood nose to nose with Nick. His fine-grained skin and bright-hazel eyes caught her attention.

A slight smirk came to his lips. "Relax. A calm perception will make your tunnel experience more enjoyable. As your spirit guide, I sympathize with your atypical day."

He fabricated total insanity. Who would go to such lengths to prank her?

The Cheshire cat grin spreading across his face ignited the sparks of nervous rage inside her from glowing kindling to a mile-high bonfire. She gripped his collar in fisted hands then twisted the ends like old rags full of dirty water.

"Tough dance auditions, traffic jams, or even a parking ticket I can handle. But telling me I'm in a waiting tunnel so you can take me to The Hotel Hereafter because I'm missing my body is pushing it. So, whatever drug you're on and gave to me is not okay. I'm pressing charges." She released him from the choke hold then examined the radiant galactic atmosphere.

Nick heaved a sigh and beckoned to some imaginary figure only he saw. "Have some tea. It will calm you. Spirit traveling is tough on the nerves, especially for you controlling types."

When a stout woman in a silver dress appeared beside her with a cup of tea, Kate held her hand up in refusal.

"Control types? I'm out of here." Only there was no exit and the passageway narrowed. Her stomach dropped. She shook like an Ewok at the *Star Wars*-like special effects swirling around her. *Run!* She ran and ran then ran some more but, like being on a treadmill, she went nowhere.

Panting with frustration, she leaned into Nick. "You've taken this joke too far and"—she frowned at the deep-orange taffeta bomb of a dress and continued through clenched teeth—"I would never wear this." She would call the police as soon as she found a phone.

"Katie." Her dad stood before her and took her hands. "I know you're scared, but you're safe, trust me. You'll remember everything. Drink the tea and rest at the hotel."

"Dad." Dreaming for sure. *Explains why I'm so foggy.* She blinked away tears of comfort and confusion at his touch. Two months ago, she'd sat by his bedside as he slipped from life to death. The cancer had eaten away at him until he existed so weak and frail, it had almost been a relief to kiss his cheek and tell him not to worry about leaving.

3

Now, he stood before her, radiating perfect health like he had never been ill a day in his life. He wore no glasses, and his hair was much thicker than she remembered, but it still showed the salt-and-pepper chapter of his middle age.

"Go with Nick," her dad said before kissing her forehead and vanishing.

"No, Dad, wait." Every muscle in her body relaxed. Her dad's presence had eased her like always.

The woman with the tea appeared again, and this time she accepted it. More time with her dad? Only a fantastic dream that made the moment all the more surreal.

Nick tossed her a stack of papers he'd pulled from his clipboard. "Your Hereafter rights, also policies and procedures. And if I had a Hereafter dollar every time a spirit traveler lost it..." He sighed. "Radical acceptance, spirit traveler. Radical acceptance."

Radical what? She'd play along for now. "So, I'm not in Heaven but the Hereafter? I'm not dead?" She sipped the last of the tea, and the cup disappeared. Where was the magician? Her eyes scanned the space around Nick.

"You're not dead yet."

"What do you mean, yet?" She moved her hand to her racing heart.

Nick led her farther into the narrow passageway, and the light became blinding. Her vision went white and, in a blink, she found herself standing in a grand hotel out of the 1800s.

The ornate lobby and dark-wood carved accents were the finest she'd seen, and, growing up in Las Vegas, there were plenty of fancy hotels. She inhaled a deep breath, and the soothing aroma of clean linens and lavender brought temporary comfort. The marble floors and crystal chandelier shone bright, and multicolored prisms danced on the walls. The plush furnishings dripping with Victorian charm caught her sight.

Silver-clad guides hustled and bustled around, handing out tea to others who apparently shared her bodiless state. An array of people from young to old congested the lobby and had her rethinking the practical joke scenario. So many people could not be part of an escapade of this magnitude.

"I realize you're still confused and most likely comprehended nothing I said. You couldn't have heard me over your internal panic rant. The tea seems to have helped."

The chamomile had to have been the strongest she'd ever tasted.

"Let me recap. You were in an accident. You'll remember soon enough." Nick handed her a manila envelope from under his arm. "Those are your medical records. Your injuries are serious, which is why you're in a coma. When near-death experiences last longer than a few seconds or hours—many do nowadays because of modern medicine—we bring you to the Hereafter. It's a place of waiting," Nick groaned, shoved by some spirit travelers making their way through the crowded lobby. "New Year's is usually busy, but this is absurd. I have others to tend to. Go over the paperwork I gave you. You'll find the answers to your questions in there."

"Hold it. I don't remember any accident, and I definitely don't feel like I'm in a coma." She wiggled her fingers in front of her face—they weren't transparent. She patted her hands over her face—yep, still felt solid, real.

"Your body is in the coma...your spirit is fine. It has the same mortal habits and sensations as your earthly body and the same human perception. By the way, we operate like Earth here. This isn't Heaven after all. Get settled and rest—it's long after midnight.

5

We'll have orientation tomorrow when everyone has had a chance to recover." Nick walked away, turning to call over his shoulder, "Out-of-body experiences often drain the soul."

She stood exhausted and with weak posture. The room—or maybe her spirit body?—swayed for a second. This had to be a lucid dream. It would explain her dad showing up and the bizarre circumstance of it all. For the time being, it kept her from losing it, so why not go with the situation?

Because she had never been one to go with the flow. As hard as she tried to accept her scenario, agitation scraped like sandpaper over her skin, and the long line she hung out in only intensified the raw feeling. How many "near deathers" could there be? And she had a list of things to do. She always had a list. Her mom needed her for something, didn't she? When would the memory smog clear?

While on the subject of making lists, changing out of the frilly, hoop-skirted ensemble should be her first item. Where had she been in such unique threads? A Halloween-themed New Year's party?

Fed up with the personal guessing game, she glanced around two tall men arguing in front of her, both clothed in leather jackets, jeans, and boots.

"This is your fault," the dark-haired, handsome one growled.

Mr. Blond-and-Striking shook his head. "Shut up."

Were they foreign GQ models? She detected the hint of an English accent from both of their tongues. *Yes, why not work some chiseled spirit travelers into the nonsensical dream?* In a flash, the loud purr of a motorcycle's engine churned through her mind without a tangible connection. One more reason to seize the moment and request an immediate transfer from the head of the Hereafter. Maybe then she'd wake up.

Assessing the crowded line, cutting would be rude and childish, but she considered a quick sprint to the front of the line before browsing through the paperwork Nick had given her. Her eyes throbbed, and she could feel a headache coming on, so she placed the sunglasses she found inside the packet over her eyes and scanned the table of contents haphazardly. Spirit food...the benefits of meditation...departments in the Hereafter.

At the slow rate the line budged, she'd be waiting for an eternity. Her pulse sped up as impatience and exasperation settled in her bones. Browsing over the different departments, she hit a dead end on how to contact God. Prayer? With a deep sigh, she closed her eyes. *Breathe.*

Out of nowhere, a gentle touch gripped her arms.

"Ashlee." A wealth of joy emanated in the name. The speaker, Mr. GQ—the dark-haired one. He wrapped his arms around her in a heartfelt embrace.

Totally awkward, being hugged by a complete stranger but comforting to be enveloped in such a loving squeeze. After all, who wouldn't need a hug in this predicament? The scent of him, a spiced warm vanilla, had her thinking maybe she should hug him, he smelled so good.

She pressed her cheek against his strong chest then let out a relaxed sigh. A moment later, she went rigid, her brain registering "stranger danger." Any minute now, he would realize his mistake and release her. Time to tell him her name was not Ashlee, but when her gaze locked with his, she stood numb.

The intense worship blazing from his eyes for his Ashlee enthralled her...would she ever get the same magnitude of smolder from a man?

He gave her a tender grin and brushed his knuckles over her cheek. "Say something, Mrs. Bennett."

Oh, she wanted to all right. She caught sight of Mr. Striking, the blond who sported a blank stare as confused as she felt. She cast a pleading gaze his way but, really, only she could set the record straight.

"I'm not Ashlee," she said, and, in a blink, tall, dark, and handsome vanished.

"Bloody hell," Mr. Striking muttered under his breath. He ran his hand through his hair.

"What the...? Where did he go?" She scanned the lobby, but he was MIA.

After a long pause, Mr. Striking spoke. "To his body, I presume. He didn't receive paperwork and told me he wouldn't be here long. He had to have been hallucinating when he called you Mrs. Bennett. You don't resemble our mum. I'm Richard Bennett," he said with an English lilt to his voice then extended his hand to her. "Are your eyes still sensitive to the light?"

She moved the sunglasses to sit atop her head and accepted his hand, not expecting the pleasant tremble up her spine his electric-blue eyes and slight grin triggered. "I'm Kate and put the shades on to stop a headache. Your mom is here, too?"

"No, she's home safe and sound. My brother, Will...I take it you didn't know him." He flipped through his paperwork.

To say good genes ran in their family, total understatement. "Nope. Who is Ashlee?" she asked when they stepped forward in line.

"No idea. Quite clear he fancies her, whoever she is." He rubbed his hand over his jaw. "Wouldn't his Ashlee be dead?"

"Or in a coma."

"Odd." He scanned his paperwork again.

Instant tranquility overtook her. What a relief to finally come down from the fear and agitation.

"Hold on. Hereafter rights should explain it." He narrowed his eyes at the paper. "Here it is. Spirits often return in the blink of an eye to the body if they live, and it's called..." He ran his finger over the paper then flipped to the next page. "Spontaneous combustion."

"He burst into flames?" Should she laugh or cry?

He gave her a grin, revealing a slight dimple. "Sorry, couldn't resist. My brother deserves spontaneous combustion but apparently experienced what's called unprompted exodus, which is what happens to a spirit traveler when they return to their body."

She raised her brows. "I'll take it over incineration."

He stepped beside her when the line moved forward again. "This has to be the most peculiar line I've ever been in."

His smooth voice sent her stomach into fidgety mode. Ridiculous. She wasn't sixteen. "It doesn't help being last."

"Right." He cocked his head and quirked a brow. "Quite a dress."

"What?" Maybe if she ignored her attire, he would, too.

He glanced over her tangled hair. "Let me guess, a New Year's party you'd rather forget?"

Time to find a rock to crawl under. "I don't remember." A skylight in her mind opened, taking her to her cousin Lyza's wedding. "I think I was a bridesmaid, maybe." She attempted to run her fingers through her mangled locks when her ring got twisted in one of the thick kinks.

"My condolences, may I?" He reached over and untwisted the knot from her knuckle.

She smiled and dropped her hand. "Thanks. I wonder if I left early, out of embarrassment. I think I did." Her cousin's wedding or not, she couldn't see herself staying in this dreaded gown longer than necessary.

"My mind's a bit foggy, too. I think I may have been out doing something. At least my brother's returned."

Lucky him. A sliver of jealousy rooted under her skin. Any moment now, unprompted exodus.

A slight breeze filtered inside from the tall, open hotel doors, and she shivered. Rubbing her hands over her arms only deepened the chill, like ice cold water freezing over her skin.

He removed his jacket and slid it over her shoulders.

"Thanks." The thoughtful act of kindness on his part charmed her.

Yes, total major challenge not to appraise his well-built physique once he'd taken off his jacket. She was only human and appreciated a fine man when she saw one. The long lean muscles of his arms and chest were superbly cut from what she could observe in his fitted black T-shirt. He was obviously athletic.

"Who's your guide?" Richard said.

"Nick. He's in demand." She searched the crowded room for the little man.

"So is my guide, Perry."

"There are a lot of"—she made air quotes with her hands—"spirit travelers."

"Yet another bizarre truth."

They stepped closer to the front desk.

"Speaking of bizarre truths, how did you take the news of this whole out-of-body experience?" she asked.

"Not well, I'm afraid. I'm not usually speechless, but this is all somewhat far-fetched. Once I could speak, I insisted Will shut up because he was yelling at Perry. Then we both drank some tea, and, strangely, all of this became much easier to accept. And you?"

She frowned. "I had a panic rant. Nick's words not mine. I may have a short fuse when it comes to finding out I'm near dead. The tea did help though."

He grinned. "Panic rant, eh? I'd say you were more than justified and, if your temper's as short as you are, I'll try and stay on your good side."

"Smart man. And you're tall."

"From your height, I suppose everyone is."

They finally approached the front desk.

"Hello and welcome to The Hotel Hereafter. I'm sorry but we're booked. Wait here and I'll see what I can do for you." The plump, rosy-cheeked woman left through a small door behind the desk before they could respond.

"Un-bloody-believable," Richard grumbled.

She wanted to collapse. To finally make it to the front of the line only to have to wait some more caused her to sway in exhaustion.

"Steady." He placed his hand on the small of her back. "You all right?"

No! "Yeah."

Starting to unravel if you want the truth. Glancing around the lobby to redirect the meltdown shadowing over her head, she observed the hush and chatter around them had settled. Only a handful of guides worked the floor, delivering blankets and pillows to the couch and chair in habitants.

"Is there another hotel?" she asked.

He removed his hand from her body. "The packet didn't mention any."

The rosy-cheeked woman came through the door. "Good news. Victoria Cottage is available. It's tiny, but being married and all, you shouldn't mind."

Kate eyed the woman's name tag. "Rose, we're not married."

Rose shrugged. "Modern couples don't always marry. I'm sorry if I offended you. You'll love the fireplace. It's perfect to cozy up to."

"Miss, we only met in line," Richard chimed in.

Rose brought her hands to her cheeks. "Oh dear, I'm sorry." She blushed. "It's all we have, as you can see." She motioned to the occupied lobby. "There really isn't anywhere else to put you. There's a loft for you," she said to Kate. "And I'm sure you wouldn't mind taking the couch, sir."

He cleared his throat. "Of course not, however—"

"Then it's settled. And really it shouldn't be longer than a few days for a room to become available here." Rose pulled the wrapper from a small piece of candy and popped it into her mouth. "Now, tell me your names, and I'll get one of your guides to meet you there and see you have everything you need."

Kate double-checked the lobby for an empty couch or chair, but they were all still taken. "One night should be fine."

"If you're sure," he said.

She nodded. He didn't have *bad guy* plastered across his forehead and, even if she miscalculated and he was a sociopath, could he hurt her if she didn't have a physical body?

Rose noted their names and who their guides were. "Thank you. I'll see which one of them can meet you there. One moment, please." She picked up the phone and talked while they waited.

Rose hung up, moved out from behind the front desk, and handed Richard a sheet of paper. "Follow the map to Victoria Cottage. Perry will greet you." She eyed Kate's dress. "Wait." Rose reached behind the desk and handed her a small bag. "A change of clothes for you. No doubt you'd be more comfortable in something else. Not much I can do about your hair." She led them out the front door before bidding them good night.

"Thanks." She moved her papers and medical records into the bag with the clothes.

Side by side, they studied the map for a few

minutes before heading down the steps of the hotel to a cobblestone path through a rose garden. Thousands of glittering stars overhead lit the way, and she stopped to gaze up at the midnight-blue sky.

He stood beside her. "Brilliant. I've never seen a greener landscape and that moon." She nodded and remembered the way her parents had described Ireland after their twentieth wedding anniversary trip. They'd shown her and her sister Kara mounds of pictures and videos, asserting the nights there had been magical, otherworldly.

"Has your memory cleared?" He studied the faded map before pointing to a narrow path.

"Not really, more of the wedding." She worked her fingers through her matted locks.

"Where?" The end of the trail opened up into a large grassy field where a tiny cottage rested on a hill.

"Mount Charleston, near Las Vegas," she told him. They hiked up the slope to the tiny house, too small for even one of the seven dwarfs. "This has to be the craziest dream I've ever had."

"Agreed. Rose should have used the word miniscule. Las Vegas?" he said as they crossed a bubbling brook over some stepping stones.

"I grew up there." She glanced over her shoulder at him.

His jaw tightened. "I was in Vegas on holiday."

"Really?" *What are the odds?* An unsettling twinge in her gut swelled. Judging from his puckered brow, something about it had distressed him, too. "What about you? Remember anything?"

"Fragmented pieces, following Will to Vegas—I'm not sure why—then being in the bright tunnel."

He lifted his hand to knock, the door opened, and a handsome dark-skinned bald man greeted them with a wide smile.

"Sorry about the tight accommodations. Kate, I'm

Perry." He stepped aside to let them in.

She struggled to get the dress to fit through the door. "Nice to meet you."

Richard ducked beneath the low stoop upon entering in order to fit through.

"Kate, Nick will meet you in the hotel lobby at eight thirty for breakfast. Orientation begins at nine. Everything you both require is here. I realize it's undersized, but it's better than the hotel floor."

"No worries, Perry," Richard assured him. "And thank you."

"Yes, thanks." She gazed up to the loft area in the shabby chic cottage. "Who lived here?"

Perry folded his arms over his chest. "Originally, the guides. The hillside used to be covered with cottages in the Victorian era. All but this one was torn down when another wing was added to the hotel. It's kind of a landmark now."

"People must have been smaller." Richard narrowed his eyes at the tiny couch before dropping his paperwork on the end table.

"It's more of a love seat." Perry sized him up then frowned. "You can always pull the cushions off and sleep in front of the fireplace. As soon as a room opens, I'll let you know. I'll see you in the lobby at eight thirty." Perry stepped out the door. "Oh, and I'm glad you two don't have any hard feelings."

Richard frowned. "Why would we?"

"Good attitude. Most would blame."

"Blame who or what?" she said.

"The car accident. Glad you two realize it wouldn't do any good to point the finger. Good night." Perry shut the door.

She lifted his jacket from her shoulders and placed it on the chintz-covered love seat. The unsettling twist in her gut tightened like a tourniquet. In a flash, her memory developed.

She dropped to the love seat.

He sat beside her.

When she recalled the shards of glass showering over her and her blood-curdling scream before everything faded to black, her mind's eye took her to the screeching brakes and the roar of the motorcycle engine. Then she came to in the bright tunnel, and Nick showed up.

"You were one of the guys racing on motorcycles." She stood.

He dropped his head. "You were the one in the Jeep."

Chapter Two
When Hell Freezes Over

When he blocked the ladder to the loft, she moved toward it. "We should discuss this."

Yes, but she didn't want to. "We should get some sleep." Was the accident her fault? It didn't matter. Sure, she could offer an apology. Then again, he may have been the one at fault. She recalled swerving, but had they drifted into her lane or she into theirs? *Say you're sorry,* get it over with.

"Get what over, exactly?" He narrowed his eyes at her.

She gazed up at him in quiet fear. "I didn't say it, I thought it. How did you know?" Had he read her thoughts?

"You said it. I heard you. Now, what is it you'd like me to do and get over with?"

"No, I thought it. Are you psychic?"

"Impossible." A slow, broad grin spread over his lips. "Then again, maybe here I am."

He can't be serious. Kind of hard to tell, with her being in a state of sleep deprivation. She lifted her chin while she studied the faded scar along his left jawline, annoyed even a scar couldn't damage his chiseled face. The polite part of her warred with the devil on her shoulder screaming, *It's his fault you're in this mess. Don't you dare apologize!*

"Apologize?" he said.

She swallowed a hefty dose of mortification. The fact he had somehow figured out how to read her mind brought her blood to a boil. Why was she attempting to spit out an apology? Hadn't she told him they should go to sleep? Whatever she uttered at this late hour would be a blend of fatigue and annoyance and all his fault.

"Isn't it why you wanted to discuss what happened, to apologize?" She tossed the bag of clothes and paperwork on the love seat. "I forgive you. Now, let's get some sleep."

"Hold on." His eyes transformed into ice-blue glaciers. "You forgive me? Which I gather means you blame me. I thought we would discuss this so you could apologize to me."

"You think this is my fault?" It could be, but no way she'd apologize now.

He shrugged. "Weren't you the one driving at hypersonic speed?"

Talk about distorting the facts. "You and your brother are obviously the reckless riders. Move." She wanted to collapse, cry her eyes out, and sleep till noon. After some rest, she would remember what actually happened and maybe prompt her body to wake up.

He stepped toward her. "I will move, as soon as you apologize."

Her lips thinned. "All right." She smiled her most innocent grin.

When he stepped away from the ladder, and she was almost halfway up it, she glared at him. "You'll get an apology from me as soon as hell freezes over."

***

What the bloody hell happened? She'd gone from a flower-crowned cherub to Satan's sidekick in an instant. He thought about her last words to him with a low chuckle, finding himself strangely attracted by her temper.

He stared up at the loft. "Would you at least throw down a blanket."

"If you send up the bag Rose gave me."

After he located the bag on the love seat and

lobbed it up, a heavy afghan landed on his head. He pulled off his shirt, socks, and boots before turning off the lights. He snatched the cushions from the couch and set them in front of the fireplace. Their earlier interaction hadn't quite gone over as he'd meant it, and, of course, he would apologize to her, whether the blame was his or not. But when she'd expected him to? Well, that had rubbed him wrong.

Placing his hands behind his head, he stared at the ceiling. What sort of enchantment had the sprite in the loft put on him? From the moment he saw her in the god-awful dress, he'd been fixated. When Will took her in his arms, jealousy had surged through him, catching him off guard. How could his affection toward her be unyielding? They were strangers to one another. But he was far too comfortable with her to call her unfamiliar. Until she'd started spewing rubbish about him apologizing.

And he couldn't be enamored by her. He still had to break off his engagement to Amber. Why hadn't he ended things before he went to Vegas? Ah yes, he'd put the deed off for the hundredth time, but to continue pretending as if things hadn't changed for him was unfair to Amber. Somewhere along the way, he'd realized he cared for her but never really loved her.

He sat up in restless agitation. As a doctor, he could handle not sleeping much, sometimes not at all. But the desire to be near Kate made this different.

Distracting himself from his interest in her, he thought to Will. What dark agenda had his brother's attention? With increasing frustration towards, and growing emotional distance from the family, Will had no resemblance to the brother he'd been raised with.

The last few years he had become aloof and cool, and, whenever he probed, Will became more of a riddle. Finally, he had decided to do some sleuthing on his own and followed him to Vegas. Funny really, he had never been a Sherlock Holmes. Sounded more like their younger brother Jack—he'd always been the clever one of the three brothers.

Will had been after someone in Vegas, but why? His obscurity and distance from the family didn't add up.

Richard's throbbing headache intensified, so he would get some sleep before he tried to figure out his brother's intentions.

And why did he want to go up to Miss Nuclear Reaction in the loft and clear up their misunderstanding? There was no denying her classic beauty, but what struck him resonated deeper than surface attraction to her dark hair, emerald eyes, and porcelain skin. However, her beauty did have him grinning from ear to ear. Her spirit, on the other hand, had her as the magnet and him steel.

Had he really heard her thoughts earlier? Could be a piece of good fortune and a nuisance. He dragged his hands over his face and fell onto the cushions. The last thing he thought about before he dozed off was the crimson color sweeping Kate's cheeks when her temper flared.

***

Only a few rays of moonlight showed through the curtains over a large window in the loft; not nearly enough to see the low-hanging sconce she ran smack into. Rubbing the knot on her forehead, she stumbled around until she found the light switch. A rosy light filled the petite loft, revealing an antique bed heaped high with satin pillows and a lacy coverlet.

Unbelievable. She tossed the afghan down to him. They both needed some time to cool down. But then why did she want to go to him and attempt a civil conversation? Fine, no denying being in his presence caused her heart to race like a hummingbird's wings, but she couldn't stop thinking about the way he calmed her nervous tension with his humor and his strong hand on her back when she swayed in the hotel lobby.

She swiped the bag from the floor and pulled out her paperwork, medical records, and finally a white cotton nightgown. First things first—time to dispose of the dress from a nightmare. Wiggling out of the poufy frock, she kicked it to the corner of the room and pulled the white nightgown over her head and petite figure. *Good riddance.*

She slumped onto the bed, strangely disappointed. Why did it have to be Richard on the motorcycle? Yes, she hardly knew him, but it would be nice to have a friend while she waited around in the Whateverafter. She sighed at the aged wood walls brushed lightly with white paint, thinking about the accident.

She shouldn't have left her cousin's reception in such a distraught state. But seeing her uncle take Lyza to the dance floor for the father-daughter dance had revealed the grief she'd been avoiding for a more convenient time. She could handle anger. At least she'd kept it simmering on low while she forgave her fiancé Rob for falling for Lyza. And maybe deep down she knew she and Rob didn't have the kind of love she would have been truly happy with, but that didn't lessen the sting.

All the drama with Rob aside, seeing Lyza with her dad opened wounds still raw. It had only been a few months since her own dad had died, and the dance reminded her of all the things she would never again share with him.

She could hear him moving around in the other room. Maybe she should go down there and tell him she hadn't meant to be rude. Nah, much easier to hide out and avoid a confrontation with the man who'd nearly killed her or who she had nearly killed.

And now, at terms with being in a coma and not dead yet, she imagined what her mom and sister were going through, worried sick over her in the hospital only a few months after watching her dad die. Way too much to contemplate, her mind wandered to her dance career. She'd lived and breathed ballet since the age of four. Would she be able to dance at the same professional level when she woke up? She shivered as a disturbing image flashed through her mind of her mangled body in the hospital.

An arctic draft in the room caught her attention, so she went to the curtains to draw them open. The window was open enough to let in the biting wind puffing hard outside. She tried to push the window shut, but it wouldn't budge.

"Come on," she muttered under her breath and hit the wood frame of the window with the palms of both hands to loosen it. When it finally started to wiggle, she pushed harder than she meant to and did an involuntary karate chop through the glass. She yelled, first in shock then in pain at the glass flying through the air that sliced across her forehead. She frowned at the jagged shard stuck in her right palm. Talk about a freak accident.

She pulled the chunk of glass out and winced at the blood. He appeared beside her in a flash.

"Let me have a look." He moved her over to the chair beside the dresser.

"I'm fine," she whimpered, holding her hand to her chest.

"I didn't say you weren't." He tilted her head to the side gently and inspected her forehead. "Give me your hand, woman."

"You do realize I have a name?"

"Give me your hand, Kate."

She pulled her hand away when he reached for it. "I'm fine. And I'm a spirit, so how am I even bleeding?"

"In the handbook, it mentions our perceptions creating situations." He glanced around the room and snatched a scarf from the nightstand. He gripped her hand in his and applied pressure.

"I'm not so good with blood." She looked down at the bright-red blotches. "It's all over my nightgown."

"It doesn't bother me." He lifted her to her feet and sat her on the bed. "We'll find you a change of clothes."

"I'll be okay," she convinced herself. When her eyes fixed on the blood-soaked scarf, the room shrank.

"Slow deep breaths," he said before she zonked out.

***

When she opened her eyes, the crisp scent of him like a sea breeze came over her. Sure, she'd noticed the ocean-spiced cologne when they first met, but it was kind of hard to overlook it now, sitting by the fireplace, nestled in his arms. Her lips were inches away from his neck. What *was* she feeling for him? It jolted her enough to wriggle away.

"Easy." He caressed her closer.

I passed out?

"Yes. How's your hand?"

She held it up and inspected the gauze wrapped around it. "Better. How did you get me down the ladder?" Did she want to know?

"Threw you over my shoulder. You don't weigh much. How's your head? Do you have a headache?"

"No." She noticed his hair was damp and perfect. He'd also changed into slacks and a button-up shirt.

How embarrassing, passing out like a fragile heroine in a gothic romance. She reached up to her forehead, feeling a small butterfly bandage. "It's so

23

cold in here."

He rubbed his hands over her arms then threw a log in the fireplace.

"This is the coziest spot in the cottage, thanks to the broken window in the loft."

The rich timbre of his voice, much to her chagrin, sent her temperature rising more than the cheerful blaze. She glanced at the robe she wore and realizing she no longer modeled the nightgown, laser-beamed him with her eyes.

"No worries." He grinned. "You have nothing I haven't seen before."

When she tightened the robe, it slid down her shoulder over her bra strap. "You make it a habit to undress unconscious women?" She pulled away from his warm hold.

"Only when they ask for help undressing, and you've been in and out of consciousness."

"I asked you to undress me?"

"Yes, uhm not exactly. You don't remember pulling the dress off? I helped you change and brought you by the fire. Hungry?"

"A little. I remember vaguely. You read to me from the handbook, something about spirit blood and our perceptions were like earth. Nick told me, I think, when I met him." She went to get up, but he stopped her.

"I'll bring you a snack." He walked to the tiny kitchen. "And you really should read through the handbook. Spirit blood is an indication of being fragile, not seeing ones' self-worth."

"Wait. You make it sound like I created it. And *you* stitched my hand?" She sat down hoping he knew what the hell he was doing. Did her hand have the stitching of Frankenstein's?

"Chapter 2 in the handbook will explain how perception and the subconscious will manifest situations. And yes, I stitched your palm." He offered her a plate of fresh fruit. "I can assure you it is not the work of Dr. Frankenstein."

"Stop it." She snatched the plate.

He sat beside her. "Stop what, exactly?"

"Reading my mind. It's rude and unnatural."

He frowned. "Maybe you should stop forcing your thoughts in my direction."

"Oh, I'm forcing my thoughts on you? Interesting, considering thoughts aren't supposed to be heard. You're in the medical field, then? Where did you get the medical supplies?" If he stitched her hand, he better be.

"I wouldn't have taken care of your wounds if I weren't. Perry brought them after you passed out. Along with a change of clothes for you. They're hanging in the loo."

She bit into a cracker. "You're a doctor?"

"Surgeon." He threw some wood in the fire.

"Thank you, then, Dr. Bennett." Best if they kept things on an impersonal level.

He narrowed his eyes at her. "My pleasure, Miss Adams."

What time was it? If she had to guess, morning, but the sky still showed dark and hardly any light came through the windows.

"After eight," he answered.

Time to get away from his X-Men-like mind-reading ability. "I'd better get ready for orientation."

He grabbed his jacket and walked out the front door without a backward glance.

***

She had given him quite a kink in his neck. He walked toward the hotel, truly exasperated by her and the hold she had over him. When had it happened?

And why did he secure her in his arms in front of the fire earlier? Frozen, he confirmed, remembering how her chilled body felt against his and also how she seemed to belong in his arms. It was far too soon to feel so right. Holding Amber in his arms never felt right.

It didn't matter. He had to end things with Amber first. His conviction to make it his first priority hit him with relief while making his way up the hotel steps.

Are you really considering a relationship with Ms. Adams, mate? He laughed out loud, surely going mad to even contemplate a ghostly rendezvous. Entertaining the idea of charming her, acceptable here because he most definitely had fallen out of his right mind. And she acted far too spiky and intolerant, right? Then again, he quite liked it. A smile fell over his lips at how she'd shifted them to a last name basis earlier. God, he hoped for a pub to appear, he needed a pint.

***

Like she was really going to an orientation for the near dead. She showered and changed into a silver dress hanging in the bathroom. With her hand covered in gauze, doing anything productive proved to be a challenge. Once she had secured her hair in a loose braid, she made herself a cup of tea, still feeling on edge, then grabbed a bagel and went upstairs to the loft to get her paperwork.

He had cleaned up the glass and pulled the curtains over the window. Freezing, she took her papers down to the cushions in front of the fireplace. She had to get out of here. No way would she keep rooming with the hottie reading her mind. Surely, there had to be someone in management able to arrange a new roommate.

Shuffling through the papers only perturbed her. Spirit travelers were to speak to their guides for an appointment with a therapist to discuss accepting their current reality. Radical acceptance she thought, remembering Nick say it to her.

As she chewed the last bite of her bagel, she snatched the homely gray sweater hanging on a hook by the front door. Maybe she'd show up at the end of the boring lecture before anyone noticed she had missed it. The cool breeze felt invigorating at first when she headed toward the hotel. But then the wind picked up and dark clouds settled above her, so she hurried her lazy pace.

She sprinted up the steps to the hotel, deciding she'd explore the hotel while everyone endured orientation.

To her relief, the lobby had no occupants. She headed past the library and down the wide hallway to a quaint shop with a sign reading Tunnel Memory Lane.

"Shouldn't you be in orientation?" a voice said.

She whirled around to the stick figure of a man standing before her. His suit was the color of polished pewter, his finger long and skeletal as he pointed toward the door. "You need to get to your therapy so we can select your bright-light tunnel-memory colors."

"Tunnel memory," she said.

He shook his head. "You haven't read through the Hereafter manual, have you?"

"I browsed." She gave him a slight grin. "So, the spirit travelers choose how they want to remember their stay?"

"Colors only. No one remembers much. The bright-light tunnel memory is all one gets, if they follow the requirements. Please get to your therapy appointment before you're too late and end up here longer than you should be." He shoved her out the door.

She wanted to live, get to earth, and on with her life, but she hesitated at following anything transporting her into her body before she knew if she would dance again or not. What could she do, ever, that would mean as much as performing had? She'd worked hard her whole life and made personal sacrifices to become a ballerina...she didn't want it any other way. She definitely needed more time to accept her uncertain future and come up with a plan B.

When she wandered down the hall and through a small door leading her behind the hotel, she saw the outdoor theatre and rushed to the platform. Thrilled at having a place to dance, she found center stage and settled into the familiar spotlight. Her body swayed into perfect form, and she leapt and glided with the ease and sophistication of a seasoned performer. Nothing else would satisfy her. The unexpected applause from Nick startled her out of her happy place.

"Missing orientation because of your love for dance I see." Nick hurried off toward the hotel.

She jumped down from the stage and ran up behind him. She felt like a child being caught ditching school. Irrational on her part because she was an adult and didn't owe him an explanation. But this suddenly felt like the longest walk she'd ever taken.

"Nick, I—"

"Better late than never," Nick cut her off and opened the hotel door. "Here are your requirements. I suggest you meet them all." He handed her an envelope. "Richard volunteered the two of you to plan our yearly dinner party for the in-the-moment assignment. It will take place a few days from now. We want you doing earthly things to occupy your time and thoughts. And the party will be a nice way to gather for goodbyes before we return you all to earth. You missed your first therapy appointment. I hope you don't make a habit of it."

She pulled the paper from the envelope. "What's the point of therapy?"

"It will help keep your spirit more connected to your body. The longer you're separated from your body, the more it's imperative you reconnect through meditation and other DBND skills. And it will help you come to terms with your uncertain future."

"DBND skills?"

Nick handed her a packet. "Dying But Not Dead strategies keep you out of emotional mind. An emotional mind can lead one to Death's Door. I'll tell you more when you come to therapy."

She choked on a laugh and glanced over the requirements paper. Step one: accept predicament wholeheartedly...*yeah right*. Step two: go to therapy...*not happening*. And Step three: in-the-moment assignment, plan dinner party with Dr. Richard Bennett...*maybe*.

"By the way, there's a nasty storm coming. Best head to the cottage soon. Let's get you some food first." Nick led her to the hotel kitchen and handed her a brown bag full of food. "It's going to be one of the biggest storms we've ever had but only tonight. See you at therapy tomorrow." He hustled out of the kitchen.

Therapy tomorrow? No thank you. As she headed toward the lobby, Richard walked up beside her and lifted the bag from her arms.

"Dr. Bennett." Why did him taking the food from her make her want to kiss him? Why did she have such fond thoughts of him all the time?

He coughed into his hand. "Curious, Ms. Adams, as to when you'd like to kiss me?"

No! Not again! She stopped and composed herself with a deep breath. "Let's get something clear. What you think you heard, me wanting to kiss you, was a kiss of gratitude." She leaned into him and kissed his cheek to prove it. "You remind me of my nerdy cousin. Thank you, Dr. Bennett." And fought the thought of how sweet his skin tasted against her lips.

He smiled. "Of course, I see you have the requirements. You know about our assignment, then?" He opened the door for her, and they made their way down the steps, a smug grin stuck to his lips.

She shrugged, pushing what seemed to be involuntary twitterpated thoughts of him aside. "We're supposed to plan a dinner party. Wasn't there anything else you could have volunteered us for?"

"If you had come to orientation like the rest of us, you could have selected something else," he teased.

She glared at him, but before she could give him a piece of her mind, it started to downpour rain.

"Here." He handed her the bag of food and removed his jacket, holding it over them both as they hurried to the cottage. Walking through the bubbling brook, she nearly tripped on the slick stones, but he moved his arm around her waist, catching her mid-fall.

They ran up the steps of the little house and rushed inside where she dropped the wet bag on the table before it ripped.

Richard ran his hand through his damp hair before hanging his wet leather jacket by the front door. Realizing she was gawking at him, she wiped the rain from her face, then pulled food from the bag.

He stepped beside her and caught her injured hand in his. "I'll have to rewrap it."

"I should put the food in the fridge first."

"I'll do it. Have a seat." His tone brooked no argument. She never liked being bossed, but her hand did need to be rewrapped.

He motioned to the chair at the small table before he put the food away then went to the couch and picked up a black duffel bag.

After a brief mental debate, she sat. "Are the

guides dead or other spirit travelers? And why is it so much like Earth here? I would think Heaven more heavenly."

He dropped the bag next to the table then inspected her hand after moving a chair to sit across from her. "Dead, and you'd know if you'd do more than browse over your paperwork. This isn't Heaven, rather a pitstop for our kind. At orientation they mentioned if they brought us to Heaven, we'd never want to live out our lives. And because we're still connected to our bodies, we still have human perceptions. Hence, your injury." He grinned. "Now, it's my turn to ask a question. Why didn't you come to orientation?"

She sighed. "I guess I'm still waiting to wake up from this bizarre dream."

"Radical acceptance not for you?"

She shrugged.

"What's wrong?"

She frowned. "I'm not sure." She stared at her hands resting on her lap. "I'm tired."

He tilted her chin up. "I'm a good listener."

Her mouth formed a weak grin. For the first time, she saw his blue eyes had bold flecks of gold in them.

His hand moved from her chin to her forehead. "Does it hurt?" He inspected her forehead when their eyes locked.

"A little."

So close she could feel his breath on her cheek, the sweet sensation had her stomach in knots.

Anxious, she shot to her feet and tripped on the strap of the black bag. When she fell against him, the force of her weight tipped him over in his chair, and they both went down.

"You all right?" He rolled her onto her back.

"Sorry." She gazed up at him and his perfect features.

"No worries." His lips held a slight grin.

A knock at the door broke the trance they were in.

He stood and lifted her to her feet. "You expecting anyone?"

"No, you?"

He shook his head, and when he opened the door, she couldn't help but notice the stunned and pleased expression he displayed at whoever stood there.

"Surprise!" a young woman shouted and leaped into Richard's arms.

"Char!" He pulled the marigold-haired blonde from his hold to assess her. "I wondered when you'd show up, little sister. Same as I remember you."

She studied his statuesque and obviously dead sister.

"Oh, Richard." Char squeezed him tight. "Or rather, Dr. Bennett."

"Yes, finally finished med school. And you're better. I'm so glad to see you in full health."

Char nodded. "Heart's as good as new here."

She could see they were close and cared for one another. So, Char had died from a heart problem, then.

"This is my sister, Charlotte." He moved to shut the door but was stopped by a woman standing in the doorway. His eyes widened on Kate then narrowed at the woman who could be her twin.

"I want you both to meet Ashlee." Charlotte motioned to her.

All Kate could do was stare as Ashlee stepped inside. The woman had brown eyes and hair only a few shades lighter than hers, but those traits appeared to be the only differences.

He shut the door. "Are you a relative of Kate's?"

Ashlee grinned. "Her and I aren't related. I'm Will's wife."

Chapter Three
Revenge

He gave a confused laugh. "Will isn't married. He swore he'd be a confirmed bachelor until, eighty, right?" He put his arm around Charlotte.

Charlotte scratched her head. "Forty, wasn't it?"

Ashlee laughed. "Yes, he told me."

"Will called me Ashlee." Kate's eyes met his.

"Right." His gaze shifted to Ashlee. "Serious? You really are my brother's dead wife?"

"Guilty."

"Why am I finding out about this now?" he asked.

"It's a long story," Ashlee said. "What happened to your hand?"

"Cut it on some glass. Will called me Mrs. Bennett, and he adored you, I mean, me as you."

Ashlee nodded. "I wish I could have seen him."

"Richard," Charlotte said. "We need to speak to you about Will."

"What's the matter with him, other than his usual rude and mysterious ways?" He motioned for Kate to sit at the table.

Ashlee sighed. "Will can be difficult."

"That's putting it mildly, please, enlighten me. I'd love to hear how you settled him down and why the family never knew about you." He pulled gauze and tape from the black bag.

"Maybe I should let you have some privacy." She stood. "I'll wait at the hotel."

He shook his head. "You're not going out in this weather. Sit."

"Please stay. This concerns you, too," Ashlee said.

She couldn't see what this Will business had to do with her, but she sat down as curiosity set in.

Charlotte went over to the fire, added some wood

then moved the cushions to the couch. She and Ashlee made themselves comfortable and watched Richard doctor her.

"See?" He removed the last of the gauze and held her hand up. "This is not the work of Dr. Frankenstein."

"No." She scrunched her nose. "It's worse."

"Really?" He started wrapping her hand.

"Maybe it's not so bad, Richard."

"We're at first names again?"

"For now."

"Oh yes," Charlotte said, and in a loud whisper to Ashlee, "This definitely involves her."

Richard and Kate exchanged curious glances.

"Afraid you're right," Ashlee whispered.

"We can hear you." He followed Kate into the sitting area. "Get on with it, then. What's going on with William?"

"Revenge." Ashlee enunciated the word with dramatic flair. Thunder boomed as if on cue.

They dropped down on the rug in front of the fire.

"What do you mean, revenge?" His brow furrowed.

"You've been following him, wondering what he's been up to. I'll tell you: revenge. A man named Cale Branson killed me," Ashlee said.

"You were murdered?" Her stomach sank.

Ashlee nodded. "Will and I became involved with each other after a mutual friend of ours, Evan, was killed. Will and I have a daughter, Madelyn. I'm worried Will's going to get himself killed, and she needs him."

He opened and closed his mouth a few times, stunned. "A daughter? I have a niece?"

Ashlee smiled. "A beautiful little girl with her dad's eyes and mischievous grin."

She didn't think she needed to know all of this. It

felt too intimate and personal. "I don't see how this concerns me."

"It may if Will's still on the road to revenge and you and my brother end up together," Charlotte said.

She snorted.

He raised a brow. "What exactly do you find so amusing?"

"We hardly know each other, and from what I did browse over in the Hereafter paperwork, we won't even remember this place once we are in our bodies. And we live in different countries."

"Out of curiosity," he spoke up. "Hypothetically speaking, of course, because of the laugh it may cause Kate, what would Will's road to revenge have to do with us?"

"If a few of the scenarios from the Hereafter statistics department come to pass, you two will meet again in England. Branson does some of his dirty work all over the UK. My naivety had me foolish enough to fall for charm over substance. When I realized his charm was a mask to hide the lunatic inside, I tried to break things off. He didn't take it with stride. On top of realizing him a creep, I learned about some shady business he oversaw. Let's say things got ugly. I met Will after Evan died...he took over where Evan left off and helped me hide from Branson. And we fell in love..." Her voice faltered.

"I'm concerned he'd think her, me. She fooled Will. Branson may hurt her because she's the image of me and possibly question if he really killed me. Branson's a sociopath—he'll have a reason."

She rolled her eyes. "Come on." The scary situation didn't have her disagreeing. The talk of scenarios and her winding up in England with the doctor were totally ridiculous. Yeah, the thought of being with him had crossed her mind. Her nervous laughter, an Adams' trait, always showed up at the most inopportune times.

"No worries on her coming to England. It is far too unlikely for her to even consider," he said.

"I never, Rich—I mean, Dr. Bennett."

"You've made it quite clear, Ms. Adams."

"She won't come to England for you because she won't remember you, but it's the deluxe déjà vu you could both experience if you guys do bump into each other concerning us." Ashlee sighed. "I'm not here to play matchmaker, but according to statistics, you two are at soul mate status. If you and Doctor Love fall for each other, and Will's still revenging, and you get caught in the middle, it could be bad."

"Hold on." She held up her hand. "We're acquaintances at best, *and* I don't date his type." Because she'd never met the man of every woman's dreams before.

He moved his mouth over her ear. "I've never been referred to as the man of every woman's dreams or Dr. Love."

She tightened her lips, fighting off a cackle. "It's crazy, the whole soul mate scenario."

Ashlee shrugged. "Maybe, but if it's even a possibility, you need to be forewarned. No, you won't remember our exact conversation, but you'll have feelings to keep you from being drawn to him if you listen."

Charlotte gestured to Richard. "As for you, we need you to go to the Department of Divine Intervention and plead for an intercession on Madelyn's behalf. The sooner you wake up, the sooner you can help Will."

"I'll do whatever I can, but how am I supposed to help Will if I don't remember any of this? He sure as hell won't tell me." He shook his head. "Will's always been too stubborn for his own good."

Charlotte shot her brother a fond glance. "And you

haven't?"

He sighed and ran his hand through his hair. "Point taken."

Charlotte sat up straight, her eyes brightening. "We can help your subconscious remember if you can convince Will somehow to stop or maybe even distract him or keep him otherwise occupied. We have to try. And you'll need to get some weapons training. Take a karate class or something."

"Please," Ashlee begged. "Madelyn's already lost one parent. She needs him."

"Right, so now I not only have to convince Will, the most stubborn and pigheaded of us, not to avenge you." He kneaded his shoulder. "But I need to sign up for spy camp on my return? I don't take lives, I save them."

"Spy camp sounds like fun for an adrenalin junkie." She had always been a fan of the 007 movies.

"I'm not an adrenalin junkie." He shot her a glare.

"Then how else did you end up here?"

"Your bat-out-of-hell driving." He narrowed his eyes at her.

"Simmer down," Charlotte spoke up. "You'll want to protect yourself, and Madelyn will appreciate having her dad around."

"I can take care of myself." She raised her chin.

"No offense"—Ashlee put her hands up—"but you're small and, while you're obviously in top physical shape, without proper training in self-defense or shooting, you'll be no match for Branson."

"I disagree." Richard rubbed his palm across his jaw. "Her sour moods alone could repel him."

Kate scowled in his direction.

"Where's Madelyn?" he asked.

"With the O'Keeffes in Ireland. We stayed at their B&B and became very close. They were like family to us. Will left her with them to follow the lead he had on

Branson that eventually led him to Vegas." Ashlee's bottom lip quivered.

Richard crossed his arms. "Why not leave her with my parents?"

"Will would never risk putting your family in danger. Branson doesn't know his true identity, but he may soon, if Will doesn't stop."

"Who does Branson think Will is?"

"Colin, the name Evan threw out before he died. Branson told him if he found me, he'd forgive Evan's debt. So, he fabricated some story about me running off with a man named Colin. And I'm glad he lied, especially once Madelyn came along."

"How old is Madelyn," Kate asked.

"Five months." Ashlee eyes swam in sadness.

"How long have you been dead?" He rubbed his chin.

"Six weeks. I died mid-November. Every day away from Will and my daughter feels like an eternity. Will's not handling it. He isn't sleeping or eating much. I've tried to reach him in dreams, but he's angry at me."

"Why would he be angry at you?" He stood.

"I left. They weren't safe with Branson after me. I did what I had to do to protect them. Once Maddie came along, my mother bear instinct kicked in. She was innocent, and worrying over my shoulder with her in my arms constantly was no life for any of us. Will and I argued about it, and I made him think I had dropped the idea, but I really thought I could convince Branson to forget about me. And I thought even if I died, it would be worth it to free them from my dilemma."

"Excuse me." She got up and walked out onto the porch where she watched the rain fall. This had nothing to do with her. Sure, she felt bad for the shady scenario her favorite doctor's family dealt with, but Richard and she were all wrong for each other…weren't they?

Ashlee walked up beside her. "I've been where you are."

"Hell?"

Ashlee grinned. "You're in love with him and you can't imagine how that's possible after knowing him just a few hours."

"You're way off. We barely tolerate each other."

"I don't think so. Be careful, if you find Richard and if you wake up. You're a tough cookie, but so was I, and see where it got me. You and him in love is probable at 99 percent from what statistics showed. Good luck denying it." Ashlee laughed when Kate opened her mouth, offended. "If he's anything like Will, you won't know what hit you. And you two make an entertaining couple." She walked down the steps and faded into mist.

You don't see someone evaporate every day. And what did she mean if I wake up? I'm waking up! Entertaining couple? She rubbed the tight knot at the nape of her neck and debated heading to the hotel's meditation room. Wouldn't she feel better after some cosmic energy flowed through her? She closed her eyes and lifted her already poised posture and began slow, deep breaths. She'd have to wait until the storm let up, she concluded then sat on the rocking chair on the porch instead, hoping he couldn't read her mind out here.

***

"I have to go." Charlotte hugged Richard.

"So soon?" He had missed his little sister for far too long. A brief conversation wasn't enough to heal the wound.

"Wake up soon. Will needs you to knock some sense into him."

"Right, because I've always been so good at getting through to him. What makes you think he'll listen to me? He never has before."

Charlotte played with her hair. "He thinks very highly of you, although he lets you think otherwise."

He fiddled with his watch. "And how do you know?"

"His guardian angel mentioned it. I can't blame you for not wanting to rush your return. Kate's lovely."

He shrugged. "I suppose."

"You should have ended it with Amber before you followed Will to Las Vegas."

"How do you know about her?"

"*Your* guardian angel." Charlotte peeked out the window to Kate on the porch. "You're frightened you won't remember her."

"I'm quite certain I'll never forget Ms. Adams. It's what has me worried." He sighed. "I don't want her anywhere near Will and this dangerous mess. Are you certain we'll meet in England?"

"As certain as anyone can be. Listen, Ashlee and I will visit after the storm passes. We'll try to squeeze you in with Divine Intervention. Will is going to feel bad about the accident and curious as to why you followed him. It will give you time to recover from your injuries and keep him off Branson's trail."

He sighed, far off in his thoughts about hearing Kate's. "I hear her thoughts at times, why?"

Charlotte grinned. "You feel a strong connection to her."

"What?" He tried to sound convincing.

"You're falling hard and fast, big brother, face it. End things with Amber. Otherwise, you'll be miserable. Not only because you're engaged to a woman you don't love, but because you won't be able to act on what you do feel for the little spitfire. I like her."

He smiled. "Don't you dare meddle."

Charlotte faded into a holographic image.

"Me? Meddle?" She blew him a kiss before disappearing in front of the door.

He grinned at the space she had occupied. He sat on the couch and rubbed his hands over his eyes. It was far too soon to feel what he did for Ms. Adams. What kind of tangled mess had Will become involved in?

"Damn," he muttered before getting up and heading to the shower.

***

When she walked inside, Charlotte had gone, and Richard was in the bathroom. Still being damp from the rain, she undid her loose braid and warmed herself in front of the fire. Running her fingers through her hair, she tried to get him out of her head. But the image in her mind showed his caring way with her and how sparks hit her lips against his cheek when she gave him the feigned-gratitude kiss. No use, she needed an intervention. She *needed* to dance. But the tiny room wouldn't allow even a half pirouette, unless she moved the couch into the kitchen and pushed the side table against the wall.

Dancing always made her forget worries. The weather had turned for the worse, so there would be no going to the outdoor theatre behind the hotel. Here in the cottage, she wouldn't get much more than a taste of motion. But at least she could try some small turns and leaps until she could return to the stage. After a few pliés and stretches, she could glide around the small space and maybe bring herself to life.

Until she came out of a piqué turn and slammed against Richard's bare chest. Her hands gripped his biceps, and her heart skipped a beat at the sight of his muscular bare chest and to the towel hanging low on him. She tilted her head up to meet his gaze.

His hands fisted against her hips. Unshaven, the one-day stubble he sported suited him.

"I like Charlotte."

He smiled down at her. "She's great."

"How old is she?"

He frowned. "Seventeen."

"Too young to die. H-how long has it been?" she stammered.

"Over ten years. I'd turned twenty and started medical school." He dropped his hands from her hips.

"Was it unexpected?" A sudden urge to extract more details about him and his family preoccupied her, and she regretted moving her hands from his biceps in that moment.

"No, we knew it was coming." His baby blues turned to dark clouds.

"I'm being nosy."

"You're fine. It's been a long time since I've thought about it is all. She's the reason I wanted to become a doctor. She had a heart condition, in and out of the hospital often. They didn't treat her as I thought they could have. I became interested in being a pediatric heart surgeon, figuring I could relate to others in the same situation. I still have a few years left in cardiothoracic residency, but it's all been worth it."

"It's a really good reason," she got out. *Great, one more cause to adore him.* And falling for the guy she collided with didn't seem like a good idea. "Guess it's my turn to shower."

"Wait." He stopped her with an arm around her waist. "You're a dancer, then? From our run-in, I assume it was your occupation."

"Ballet, New York."

"Impressive."

The word she would use to describe his physique.

A wide grin spread over his lips.

Mind-reading Doctor of Lust. "I'm going to shower." She darted to the bathroom.

A room had better turn up at the hotel soon. The more time she spent with him in close quarters, the more likely her attraction to him would grow. She peeled off her dress and stepped into the cool shower.

***

Hours had passed since she'd danced into his towel-clad body. And much to her great relief, he had put his jeans and T-shirt on. True, he carried the casual wear off like a GQ model, but that was more bearable than him being half-naked.

They'd successfully avoided each other after lunch. He napped in front of the fire while she went up to the loft and gathered her paperwork. It was far too cold to stay up there, but staring at Dr. Bennett in front of the fire? Not an option.

And wanting anything more than friendship with him? Bad idea. He would only distract her from the goal of getting out of the dream and off to reality. Although, his bedside manner, the complete opposite of what she'd experienced with her dad's self-absorbed doctors, had already won her over. Her dad had been in and out of the hospital and treatment center often enough for her to get a bad taste in her mouth at the sight of the building. She'd never cared for doctors...until now.

His kind eyes and genuine concern had done it—made her think about and reconsider her bias. Becoming a doctor because of his little sister wasn't too shabby, either. She imagined him in scrubs. The vision brought a wide smile to her lips and sent her heart beating like a hammer. Enough. She reminded herself as a grown woman, not a boy-crazy teen, she could handle it. And besides, she'd only known him less than twenty-four hours, going into their second night at the cottage.

She went to the kitchen and assessed the ingredients Nick had given her earlier. Having all of the items for chicken soup, she started dinner then brewed a pot of peppermint tea and sat at the table and watched the rain turn to snow.

What little light peeked through the clouds vanished. The sky turned from dusk to midnight all at once. She flipped the kitchen switch, expecting illumination, nothing happened.

Going to the other switches in the sitting room, she got the same no-shine result.

He woke from his nap and sat up. "Still raining?" He stood then stretched.

"It's a blizzard now. What is with the ever-changing weather here?" She grabbed the two candles from the mantel and went to the kitchen to light them.

"It's like this once a year in January. They mentioned it at orientation. Should clear sometime tomorrow before the next storm comes around again." He lit some more candles and brought them to the table and sitting area. "We should start on the dinner party plans. It's in two days."

"I still don't see the point of this. It's like we're stuck in a twisted version of summer camp and we've been assigned to be the activity directors. Life is stressful enough. I thought the Hereafter was supposed to be a place of tranquility."

"Those who skip out on orientation can't complain about the Hereafter rules." He smirked. "Every spirit was assigned some task or activity to plan. As for tranquility, that only counts when you're permanently dead."

"It's a good thing I jotted down some ideas while you were sleeping." She handed him her notes.

He picked up an apple from the counter and bit into it, glancing over the paper. "This is hardly legible, worse than mine. Doctors are known to write sloppy, but I'd expect better penmanship from a ballerina."

"What?" She jerked the paper from his grasp.

He winked. "I'm kidding." He plucked the paper from her fingers. "Moonlight Cove, eh? I saw it on the map."

"The map described small holes in the ceiling of the cave, lets in the moonlight, and there's a waterfall. It should be warm in time for the party, according to your weather prediction earlier."

He bit into the apple. "As long as there's an area large enough for dinner and dancing, any ideas on a theme?"

"The only thing I can think of is something with color. No silver."

"Right, as I recall from your dress last night, you do prefer showy."

She bit her lip, horrified frou-frou would always be his first impression of her. "My cousin chose the dress."

"Your cousin must be blooming mad."

She choked on a laugh. "Maybe, but she's still my cousin. The dinner plans, any other ideas?"

"I suppose a theme will come to us when we have the location. Near the sea perhaps, candles on tables with large draped settings and bright colors."

She grinned. "Do you decorate in your spare time?"

"No. My parents have dinner parties regularly. I've been to enough to know how it's done."

Was he English royalty? A lord or a duke? A wry grin came to her lips at her daydream before she shrugged off the idea.

He cringed. "Not in the slightest. My father's businesses keep my parents in social circles quite often." He went to the teeny fridge and grabbed a soda. "Do I act like royalty to you?"

She glared at him. "Considering I thought it and didn't say it, yes, a royal pain in the—"

He laughed. "I asked for it."

"I'll say. Is there anything in the Hereafter packet about mind-reading doctors?"

"Strangely, no, but Charlotte did mention something about it."

"What?"

He shook his head. "You'll laugh or start referring to me as Dr. Bennett again."

She bit her lip to stop her snicker. "I promise not to laugh or get too formal."

"All right, then." He swayed on his feet. "She said I must feel a close connection to you."

"Oh, interesting." And appealing, she decided as the teenager inside her jumped up and down, waving pom-poms, and doing back handsprings. Maybe she should make the first move. Then again, being forward wasn't really her style. "Um...so, you mentioned earlier you knew how dinner parties were done. Do we have the resources for draped tables and candles?" She went to the fireplace and warmed her hands in front of the rising flames.

"Yeah, Perry mentioned if we get everything to him and Nick by tomorrow, they can have whatever we need ready."

"Great." She wondered what his dad did for a living. "So, your dad owns businesses?"

He set his drink on the carved wooden mantel. "Yes."

"What kind?"

"A hotel and jewelry chain to name a few."

She rubbed the spot on her wrist where her favorite charm bracelet usually hung. But she hadn't worn it for the wedding; maybe that was why it was missing.

"Missing something?" He eyed her wrist.

"A charm bracelet."

"What kind of charm bracelet?"

"It has pink sapphires and a gold ballet dancer charm. My parents got it from Crown Caroline when I became a lead dancer. They saved up for a year to buy it. I don't really like fancy jewelry but it means a lot to me."

A fox's grin came to his lips as he added more wood to the fire. "Crown Caroline, you don't say."

"Your dad owns Crown Caroline?"

"Yes. How long have you danced?"

"Don't change the subject."

He grinned. "I'd rather discuss you, not my father's businesses. How long have you danced?"

His dad must be a wealthy man. "I was four when I started," she mumbled. Would she ever dance again?

He stepped away from the mantel and in front of her. "You're sad."

She puffed her cheeks at his psychic ability.

He put his hands up in defense. "Your face says it all. No mind reading, I promise."

"I miss it."

"Dancing?"

She nodded. "I'm not used to sitting around, waiting for storms to pass. If I can't dance when I wake up..." She held her breath then exhaled. "I don't understand my medical records, and if I'm hurt badly enough to be in a coma, then my dance career could be at stake."

"May I have a look at your paperwork? Perhaps I can ease your mind."

But he couldn't. What doctor had ever eased her dad's mind? She would never forget her dad's face the day they told him there was nothing more they could do for him and to get his affairs in order.

"It's better if I don't know, Doctor, but thank you."
She wished she could take her stiff tone of voice back.

"Are we at the doctor rubbish again?"

"You *are* a doctor, and we really don't know each
other."

He gazed up in agitation. "No, I suppose we don't.
But your thoughts suggest you'd like to get to know
me."

Her skin tingled with the burning sensation of
third-degree embarrassment. "Soup should be ready."
She turned on her heels and fled to the kitchen.

***

A broad grin spread over his lips. Probably best to
avoid the topic. It wasn't like he could act on his desire
for her...not yet. He followed her to the kitchen, with
hopes of hearing more of her thoughts.

Chapter Four
Fictional Love Affair

They ate in silence while they both surveyed menu ideas for the party. She refrained from shooting laser beam glares at Doctor Smug. The arrogant grin plastered to his lips had her contemplating shoving him outside and locking the door. Maybe a good snowstorm would shrink his massive ego.

Then again, as much as she hated to admit it, she knew he had no big ego. Maybe he liked to take things slow.

After they finished dinner in awkward avoidance, he moved their bowls to the sink and washed the dishes.

She searched around for cards, books, magazines, anything to distract her mind and keep her thoughts safe from the resident psychic. Nothing turned up in her desperate search, so she cleaned the bathroom then went over to the fire, added some more wood, and watched it crackle and hiss. A heavy sigh escaped her, bored with studying knickknacks on the mantel. Glass-blown vases, lace doilies, and a few candlesticks made her think to her grandma Mary's antique collection. Her eyes stopped on a light-brown and turquoise bound book. She lifted it off the mantel and dropped to the floor in front of the warm hearth.

"What did you find?" He sat beside her.

"I thought it was a book, but it's a journal." When she flipped through the pages, a letter fell out.

He snatched it. "Let's hope it's more interesting than the Hereafter rules and regs." He opened the letter.

She inspected the pages. "Most of it's blank, but it's short correspondence between..." She squinted. "I can't read the name on this, but I think it's Clair." She held it up to his face.

He tilted his head and pressed his lips together. "Yes, and she's addressed this letter to a Mr. Grant. And it's dated..." He narrowed his eyes. "The last part's faded, eighteen something."

"A long time ago."

Richard cleared his throat and read.

Mister Grant,

It is with great disappointment and a heavy heart that I write this letter to you. I can no longer see you and would appreciate your cooperation in this matter. As your guide, it may have been wrong for me to allow such a close relationship to exist between us, and, therefore, your new guide will come promptly for you tomorrow morning to make sure you understand everything before returning to your life on earth. I shall always think fondly of you, my dearest Jonathan, even though you won't remember me.

Yours Affectionately,
Clair

He folded the letter and handed it to her. "Cruel."

She stared at him unable to respond. His accent and voice had been like a sweet trance.

He nudged her. "You okay?"

She blinked. "It's sad." More like pathetic her response to him came so unmanaged.

He lifted the journal from her lap. "Quite." He flipped through the pages and found another letter. "This one is addressed to Clair."

"We shouldn't be reading these." She slumped her shoulders.

"You're right."

She bit her lip before rationalizing. "Then again, it was here on the mantel. Clair or Mr. Grant should have hidden the book from plain sight." She stood and paced.

"So?" He stood in front of her when she stopped pacing.

She gazed up at him. "Read it."

"Thought you'd never ask."

Clair,

I've searched everywhere for you after receiving your letter. I have decided to appeal my life certificate. We belong together. Going to a life without you would not be living at all. My new guide has delivered the paperwork to Divine Intervention, and so I sit here in this cottage, thinking of you and the time we spent here together with great fondness. I'll be waiting for you in Moonlight Cove at midnight. If you do not come, I will only then stop pressing this issue. And I do not believe I shall ever forget you as you say I will.

With Love,

Jonathan

He tucked the letter in the envelope.

"There has to be more." She searched the small journal for clues to the outcome of this couple's predicament. She fanned herself, wondering how it could be so hot? Maybe she should have read the second letter. It would help if Richard didn't talk much. How could she get him to stay mute so she could think like an adult and not the president of his fan club?

He handed the envelope to her. "Do you think she went to Moonlight Cove?"

"I hope so." She went to the kitchen, poured some juice, and offered a glass to Richard. He nodded and walked toward her. "If not, he had to have been upset."

They brought their juice to the couch.

He sat next to her. "Would you have gone to him?"
"Yes."

She found herself enthralled with the cadence of his voice, the way he paused for effect on certain words, and his overall opinion of the love affair.

"Doomed from the get-go," he finished.

"You don't find it romantic?" She leaned forward.

"Yeah and tragic but very negligent on her part."

She straightened. "What?"

He laughed. "You're so quick to anger. Relax. I'm joking." He pulled her beside him. "No worries. I'm sure he saw her when he died later in life. Perhaps they're together now."

"Maybe." She liked his version of how it ended. It made sense. Wouldn't Jonathan look for Clair when he died? Kate undid her braid and ran her hands through her hair. An awful thought occurred to her. "What if he was married?" She turned to him.

He frowned. "A possibility."

She picked up the journal and searched through the pages.

He nudged her with his shoulder. "Glaring at it again isn't going to make another letter appear."

"There has to be more written in the journal." She scanned over notes and the chapter headings of a few pages. "No." She crinkled her nose.

"What?"

"It's fiction. Someone here before us decided to write a book. They even wrote Clair and Jonathan's letters in different handwriting."

He pulled the journal from her hands. Flipping through the pages, pausing here and there to read them over.

"I feel slighted. Nothing but notes and ideas."

He handed the journal to her. "You're making it difficult to stay upset with you about the accident."

She knew the feeling and, for a moment, bathed in

the warmth of his eyes. "Let's just call a truce for now."

"I am sorry, Kate. I don't remember much, but I recall it being my idea to race Will. I thought once I won our race, he'd give me answers as to who he was after in Vegas."

She bit her bottom lip. "No, I'm sorry. The accident is still a blur, but I know I drove under a strain."

"What were you upset about?" he nudged her.

She didn't want to talk about it but then turned to him, ready to tell him about her dad.

He jolted up and snatched two folded blankets from the couch. "Maybe we can discuss it another time."

"Where are you going?"

"The loft."

"It's freezing up there." She walked up to him and shivered when the chill air hit her. "Afraid you won't be able to keep your hands off of me?" A girl could dream.

He slowly moved the strands of hair that had fallen over her eyes behind her ear. "Yes. Good night."

***

She hadn't expected such a blunt answer. Or for his honesty to send warm shock waves through her. It had to be Clair and Jonathan's fictional love affair that had her all worked up.

Half an hour passed, and she wanted to check on him. She shouldn't worry. *Could a spirit freeze to death?* It sure felt like it. And passing the time proved harder alone. She sat on the couch with the journal and flipped through it again. She stopped on the page titled Last Chapter, it was blank. Disappointed to be left hanging, she scanned the room in desperation for what to do.

***

He sat on the tiny bed and wrapped the two blankets around him. Better to risk freezing than spend too much quality time with Kate. And why had he been so direct? He didn't want to lie to her and considered telling her about Amber. Hearing a few of her thoughts gave him a hint she could have feelings for him. But he would have to know for sure before he mentioned his fiancée. Was he really contemplating such things, or was it wishful thinking on his part?

When his teeth started to chatter, he realized, with the broken window in the loft, hiding from her may be hazardous to his health. And it couldn't hurt to talk to her, get to know her better. Find out what had her upset the night of the accident. From what he'd seen and how she'd handled things, he quite liked her...independent and strong. She definitely had her own ideas about everything, and he found it quite refreshing to listen to her opinionated views. Amber had been far too agreeable about everything.

Reluctantly, he stood and let the blankets fall to the floor. He let out a long sigh. "Alright, mate, time to face Ms. Adams." And down the ladder he went to find her doing some bending exercise dancers did.

***

"Have you always wanted to dance?" he asked, standing at the bottom of the ladder.

She nodded his way. "It's all I've ever done." She stopped stretching.

"I've been to the ballet a few times, unwillingly of course." He moved in front of the fire.

"Of course." She smiled. "I've never been to England." She'd thought about visiting someday. "I had a dance teacher from England, Judy. We still keep in touch."

"Maybe she's what brings you to the U.K. According to what Ashlee mentioned could happen, I mean."

Made sense. "Okay, but we're talking about something I haven't done yet. Doesn't it seem strange to you?"

"Absolutely, but being where we are, I've come to accept the strange as acceptable."

Shaking her head at him, she smiled. "How do you do it?"

He grinned. "What?"

"Accept all of this and stay so calm."

"In my nature, I suppose. And it's yours to question everything, right?"

She picked up a blanket from the couch and moved beside him to stand in front of the fire.

"Maybe." How did he know that about her already?

"Where in England does Judy live?"

"Cornwall. Where do you live?"

"Cornwall."

A notable coincidence, she thought. "Hmm, she comes to New York often. I'm sure I won't be going to England." She couldn't entertain the idea of her and Richard. Way too far-fetched. What did the statistics department here know anyway? Her mind wandered to his brother and the dangerous scenario Ashlee and Charlotte had explained to them. "You must really care about Will to follow him to Vegas. Why did you follow him?"

Disappointment settled over his face.

"It's none of my business."

He threw some more wood into the fire. "I don't mind discussing it with you. He upset my mum for the umpteenth time because of his absence, and I didn't buy his story of what always kept him away. I started following him, and when he booked a commercial flight, it didn't add up. Our family has a private plane, so it made sense to me he obviously had something to hide. And honestly, I'm not sure how I feel about my big brother. He's been detached from me and the rest of our family for years. It makes a bit more sense with his secret wife and child situation. Has to be why he's stayed clear of us for so long."

"Right, to protect you all from the Branson guy. Is your brother an agent or something?" She pushed the couch closer to the fireplace.

He helped her then they sat. "No, but who knows as, apparently, I've been out of the loop for some time? He was in the British army when he was younger and had aspired to take over the family businesses for our father but then declined. My father couldn't understand it; none of us could really. Will's a savvy businessman. Jack, our younger brother, stepped in to fill Will's place. He's doing a fine job but wanted a more low-key position."

So, he had two brothers. She thought about Ashlee. "And Will's obviously mourning Ashlee. I feel bad for him."

"Yeah, his dark mood makes sense now. I understand him wanting to go after Branson, but with a daughter...he should be more careful."

She nodded and leaned closer to the fireplace. "Do you think you'll wake up soon?"

"Hard to say. I wouldn't bet my life on it." He grinned. "Speaking of gambling, you much of a gambler growing up in Vegas and all?"

"No, and a little presumptuous?"

"I suppose. How was growing up in a place like Vegas?"

"Good, great actually. We lived nowhere near the strip and only went when relatives came to visit. It's different now, for me anyway."

"Your dad, it's what you were upset about the night we collided."

She gave him a scowl but felt tempted to talk to him. Like he'd maybe understand how losing her dad had changed her and how the sad memories kept her away from home.

"By the grimace on your face, I read your mind again. Do your parents still live in Vegas?"

"My mom does."

"Divorced, then?"

"My dad died a few months ago." She fought back tears.

"I'm sorry, how?"

"Cancer."

"It's hard to watch anyone suffer, especially family. Has he come to you yet?"

"In the tunnel for a minute." She sighed. "It's still hard to believe, him dying I mean. I never thought he would. I somehow convinced myself he'd beat it."

"I know what you mean. With Charlotte, I thought the same thing. She lived with a frail and tired body but such a spunky soul. A lot like Will in the mischievous department. Seeing her sick so often devastated me, I felt helpless."

"Me, too."

"Did you have much time with him? Once you knew he had cancer I mean."

"He lived longer than the doctors predicted. Years after he was misdiagnosed."

"Misdiagnosed?"

"Yeah, we had a nasty trial before I graduated high school."

"I assumed it an honest mistake."

"No." She couldn't believe how comfortable she felt telling him all of it. She hadn't discussed her dad's situation with anyone. "The doctors got away with it, figuring my dad would die anyway. My parents got a settlement, and it eased my dad's worries about the medical bills piling up."

He put his hand on hers. "I'm sorry, Kate. It all sounds dreadful."

She squeezed his hand. "You're a good doctor. I'm not used to good doctors. My dad became a statistic, little if any compassion, only the facts of the diagnosis and a guinea pig for experimental drugs." Her bitterness caused her voice to almost break.

He nodded. "I know the types. Charlotte was treated by many like you describe. Unfortunately, I work with a few doctors similar, but then there are a lot of good ones. I suppose there are bad apples in every profession though."

She blinked through the puddle of tears threatening to fall. "It shouldn't have happened."

He moved his arm around her. "Grief's different for everyone, and there's no timetable for getting over losing someone you love. You miss him; it hurts. Something tells me you're not the crying type. It would do you good."

She lowered her head to look at her lap so he wouldn't see how close she was to doing exactly as he'd suggested. "The night of the accident I left my cousin's reception. When she danced with her dad, I lost it and fled. Not very mature, I know." She looked up and caught his gaze with hers.

"Don't be so hard on yourself." He frowned. "It' understandable, you were upset because you'd never have the moment with your dad."

"I drove through a massive panic attack. I hit you and your brother. It's my fault. I should have pulled over and calmed down." The details were still hazy, but it had to be her fault.

"Hopefully, some sense was jolted into Will, and, honestly, I can't remember details. It doesn't matter. If we follow the requirements, we'll wake up."

Coming to and not remembering him seemed cruel. She stood. "It's late. We'll be busy tomorrow with party plans. The storm should be over by morning."

He moved the couch away from the fireplace, pulled the cushions off, and tossed them on the rug. She made a bed for herself then headed to the ladder to grab the blankets he had taken into the loft.

"I could have fetched those." He rubbed his hand over his neck.

"I don't mind." Being nice to him was easy again. She made a bed for him beside her. "You'll be warmer here."

"Thank you." He gave her a slight grin.

"You're welcome." She huddled under the blankets and faced the fire.

When he lay beside her, she felt like a teenager waiting for the guy to make the first move. She wanted to be in his arms, not beside him. And she longed to ask him questions, all night if he'd allow it. *For starters, how old are you, twenty-nine or thirty? What did you do when you weren't saving lives? And most importantly, do you like brunettes?*

Please don't hear my thoughts. She closed her eyes and repeated it over and over.

***

He could hear her thoughts all right. Her mind moved quickly and most likely contributed to him only ever getting a few snippets here or there. As he saw it, he had two options. The first being to believe this was all a dream and act on his feelings for her. To take her in his arms now and tell her whatever she asked of him. More than anything, he wanted to caress every part of her and show her what she did to him. His heart raced in anxious anticipation.

However, the second option had him bitter and cursing his moral nature. He would regrettably have to hold off kissing her from head to toe because he knew this dreamlike series of events was all too real, and he still had a fiancée to break things off with.

He shifted his body to face hers, and a twinge of devastation hit him at greeting her back. Still, it prompted him to lean close, his lips over her ear, and whisper that the only brunette he adored was her. A deep sigh escaped him when he sat up instead.

"Kate, I..." He paused, on the brink of telling her he wanted her in his arms.

"What?" She about-faced to him.

He smiled regrettably, knowing the time would come. "I don't need two pillows." And he handed her one.

Chapter Five
Sea Breeze and Cupcake

In the morning, a lazy grin came to her lips when she realized Richard's arms held her in a cozy, sheltered dreamy embrace. Inhaling the crisp, sandy beach scent of him had her thanking her subconscious for the most lucid fantasy ever.

"You smell like the beach," she mumbled.

"What?" He pulled her closer.

"A warm sunny day, sea breeze, you," she whispered, never wanting to wake from the delusion.

He laughed and covered her with the blanket wadded up behind her. "You don't say. Strawberry cupcakes."

"Mmm." She thought that sounded good.

"You smell like strawberry cupcakes."

"What?" She sprang up.

He sat up on his elbows. "You heard me, Cupcake."

She laughed. "I thought I was dreaming." She stood with the blanket wrapped around her. "Wait." She went to the window, drew open the curtains, and smiled at the bright rays dancing in the room.

"It's like it never stormed." He stood beside her. "Now, we can get out and explore Moonlight Cove and the sea."

"I'll clean up." She picked up a blanket to fold but he stopped her.

"Easy, don't want to loosen your stitches. I can handle this."

"I'll shower, then."

"Chocolate chip pancakes sound good?

"Sounds great, need some help?"

He shook his head and nodded toward the bathroom. "I've got it."

She went to close the bathroom door but left it cracked enough to watch him fix breakfast. He seemed at ease in the kitchen and why not add culinary skills to his Mr. Perfect persona?

He ate while studying the map and then she watched him set some aside for her, then he packed a lunch for them. A picnic near the sea with the most handsome guy ever would be nice after being cooped up during the storm.

He found a basket in the loft, and, after setting it on the counter, he strategically placed the sandwiches, cheese, grapes, and teacups inside. He left the bottle of peach wine on the counter beside it.

When she realized she had eavesdropped on him long enough, she showered and attempted to make herself irresistible to him with at least 3 different hairstyles and then gave up at the ridiculous effort. She shook her head and got dressed then stepped into the kitchen.

She hoped the sunlight highlighted her dark hair with gold streaks and made her eyes seem much lighter than the emerald green they were. Isn't that how the hot guy in a novel adored the fair maiden? Help, she needed psychiatric help.

Richard grinned over at her with that knowing look.

Please no! Had he heard that ridiculous mind chatter?

"Here you are." He cleared his throat and set the plate of pancakes on the table with some juice then pulled the chair out for her.

"Thank you."

He smiled and nodded before heading to the loo.

Kate took the first bite. If Richard continued on with his kind and considerate ways, she would be tempted to nickname him Prince Charming. And wasn't he though? Rob had never made her a meal or pulled her chairs out for her, come to think of it. He proved to be chivalrous and made the best pancakes she'd ever tasted.

She rinsed off the dishes, and when he came out of the bathroom, dressed in the slacks and white shirt, she hurried to appear busy tidying up so as not to stare at him.

"Ready?" He pulled the map from the counter and studied it. "We'll need to get a horse and buggy, behind the hotel. Too far to walk to the beach." He shrugged. "Then we can head to Moonlight Cove after, if it's all right with you?"

"Yeah, horse and buggy, no cars?"

"Not here. Quite like it."

She nodded. A car *would* feel out of place here.

He picked up the basket off the counter then grabbed the wine, and they walked to the hotel. She smiled at the sight of others out enjoying the day. A man with a black beret caught her attention. He painted on a large piece of canvas, and she and Richard paused in unison to examine it. The image of the hotel he'd created brought both abstract and bright, Monet-like figures to life around the steps.

He touched her arm and pointed past the garden to a carriage. "There's our ride."

When they walked to it and Richard had set the basket in, he motioned for her hand and helped her in then sat beside her. The small bench forced them right up against one another. When he loosened the reins, the horses clip-clopped off at a steady pace. They passed through a thick grove of trees and into a wide-open field of red and orange flowers lining the dirt road they traveled on. The smell of wet jasmine filled the air.

She turned to him. "Listen, I know the Clair and Jonathan letters and journal was a story, but it got me thinking. We should do a Victorian theme, give it a late

1800s feel. Maybe mix in some modern music with classical for the dancing part of the evening."

"Sounds perfect. We need to decide on a menu though. What do you think of a roast and salad with pastries for dessert?"

"Works for me." She squinted at the bright sun, and when the ocean came into view, she couldn't believe how quickly the field of flowers turned into a sandy beach.

Richard pulled on the reins and steered the carriage to the side of the road.

After setting the brake and assisting her out of the carriage, he tucked his hands into his pockets as they headed toward the beach. Once on the sand, she kicked off her flats and walked toward the waves while he removed his shoes.

"This could definitely work," she told him when he caught up.

He surveyed the area. "We'd want to keep everything in close proximity, tables grouped in one spot, the dance floor not too far from it. I'll be counting on you to show me how to dance. I'm a bit clumsy."

She found it hard to believe he had awkward dancing abilities but agreed to help him. Why did she have to find him so charming? The timing was so off. They weren't even awake!

He talked about appetizers; she heard him but didn't pay attention to his words. His accent and voice had her in another embarrassing trance and she sighed when the melancholy set in.

"So?" he pushed.

"What?"

"Am I boring you?"

She gazed at his lips. "I'm thinking of something else."

"Care to share? My mind reading is a bit off."

Halleluiah for that.

A wave of sadness came over her for both of their families, worrying about them at the hospital. His perfect lips had brought guilt up for her again. What if she was somehow responsible for scarring his lips she so badly wanted to kiss?

"I was just thinking about us, about our bodies I mean." That came out wrong.

He smirked. "Sorry?"

"I mean the accident, it obviously messed us both up. Your parents must be worried sick. I mean, Charlotte is dead, and you and Will are seriously hurt. My mom and sister, it has to bring up losing my dad since it's only been a few months. And here we are, spirit travelers. I'm thinking too much I guess."

He licked his lips. "I've wondered about our families. It would be nice to let them know we're still aware."

They listened to the waves roll over the sand and she shook her head, letting go of the thoughts she couldn't do anything about until she woke up.

"The dinner party, we might want to change the theme. Victorian attire on the sand could be tough."

"True, but I'd hate to." He stopped and leaned against a large rock. "This place reminds me of Lusty Glaze."

Had she heard that right, lusty? "What?"

"Lusty Glaze, it's a beach not too far from where I live."

Of course he would live somewhere lustful. "It must be beautiful."

He started to laugh and then coughed. "It is. I go there on my days off, read and unwind."

Was she really entertaining thoughts of what she would do with him at Lusty Glaze?

He gave her a smoldering stare. "Tell me, Kate, what *would* you do with me at Lusty Glaze?"

No, no, no! Everyone has random thoughts pop

into their head about things they'd never do or consider doing, why did he have to hear hers? "I'll go get the basket you packed. I'm hungry." When she beelined for the carriage, he stopped her by taking her arm.

"I'll go after it." He hurried off.

She wandered toward some large rocks forming a near-perfect circle. Did she need to sign something to keep him from hearing her thoughts? Unanswered prayers department maybe? Why hadn't she paid more attention to the Hereafter rights? Maybe if she dug fast, she could bury herself beneath the rocks.

He returned in record time and spread out the blanket he had under his arm. "Found the blanket in the carriage."

He set out the food from the basket and handed her a teacup when she sat beside him on the soft coverlet.

After he poured them some wine, they ate in silence. It wasn't awkward at all, but she wondered if he felt the same urgent desire to move closer, hold hands, and kiss. The random thoughts kept popping up in her mind and making her edgy.

Richard rested on his elbows, and his eyes caught hers. "I'd like to discuss these random thoughts of yours making you edgy." He raised his eyebrows. "I'd like to ask you something."

"Can't you just read my mind?"

"Not often enough to know what I'd like to."

She jumped to her feet and rushed toward the water, lifting the long dress up so it wouldn't get drenched.

He jogged up beside her.

"What did you want to ask me?" she blurted.

When a warm breeze blew her hair over her eyes, he stepped in front of her and tucked her hair behind her ear. "What exactly is it you feel for me, Kate?"

She shook her head, unable to speak. Emotional circumstances like this, brutal; like pulling teeth without pain meds. She couldn't tell him how frightening the thought of waking up had her because she'd never see him again, the fixation on him consuming, too much, too soon, and the most alive she'd ever remembered existing—ironic, her being near dead and all.

"Isn't it obvious?" She glanced up at him.

He gave her a slight grin. "I suspect it's more than cousinly affection but would like to hear it from your lips instead pieces of your thoughts."

Her first instinct? Run, fast and far, only because losing him scared her to death. But she didn't really have him, did she? She'd known him what, a few days? She'd have to show instead of tell him because words never came easy for her to express her feelings.

"I don't want to forget you," she whispered.

"I'm quite sure I could never forget you."

There was that look of his, the one where his eyes touched her soul and made her feel like the most beautiful woman ever to walk the earth and prodded her to spring into his arms and kiss him. Yes, she'd lost it.

Her sudden move knocked him off-balance, and they fell into the water, her landing on top of him. It shouldn't have been a perfect kiss but it held true. They were both laughing and the salty warm water got in their mouths and eyes, and she felt exhilarated, she felt whole. The kiss washed away all the pain of the last year, her father's death, Rob's betrayal. It occurred to her breaking off their engagement had actually been a gift. She knew now, settling for Rob would have been the worst kind of mistake. And she knew, in a place way beyond words, being with Richard was where she was meant to be.

The sea spray rose around them, and, as they held

one another, it didn't seem encompassing enough. When they paused for a breath, she rested her head against his shoulder. "Answered your question."

He kissed her neck.

"You feel the same, I guess?" She gripped his wet shirt.

He kissed her, long and mind-spinning then pulled away from her in slow motion. "Is that clear enough?" he whispered.

She could only nod.

"I have to tell you something." He lifted them to their feet. "It's really a minor technicality and makes me wish I'd taken care of it sooner."

"What are you talking about?" She unwrapped the soggy bandage from her hand.

"It's healing nicely." He caressed her hand. "I'm going to say this, get it out. Then we can discuss it."

"Okay. Were you in prison or something?"

He gave her a weak grin. "Of course not, your imagination is quite remarkable. Look, I never expected to more than tolerate you. I figured the thing I have to tell you wouldn't matter."

"Tolerate me? How sweet," she teased. "Did I annoy you that much?"

He shook his head. "You bothered me, love, but in a very good way. From the moment I saw you, you have held my every thought." He kissed her.

They dropped to the sand, and he rolled her onto her back and then pulled away and sat up.

She moved next to him and rested her head on his shoulder. "Is it that bad?"

"Yes and no. It's your reaction to what I'm going to tell you, I suppose, that has me most reluctant."

They sat for a long while in silence, and she nestled her face into his neck when he pulled her into his arms.

"Just say it." She tried to ignore the knot in her

stomach.

"Right." He pulled them both to their feet. He took her face in his hands. "I'm sort of, I guess it's best to blurt it..." He took a breath. "I am engaged."

"Engaged?" She stepped back and shook her head. In an instant, her blood pressure shot to an explosive level.

"Yes, please, just hear me out."

"Hear you out?" She walked away, agony in every step away from him.

"Kate, I know you're upset."

She stopped and gave him a glare that burned her eyes. "You're engaged, which means this, *us*, doesn't matter." She shot toward the horse and buggy.

"Kate!" He ran after her.

She turned around and put her hand up. "Why did you have to kiss me?"

He froze. "Technically, you kissed me."

"You kissed me back and shouldn't have."

She backed away from him, jumped into the carriage, and raced off. He could walk the long road to the hotel and find himself a room. She was too mad to cry or scream. Why hadn't he told her sooner? She drove the carriage at top speed then stopped in front of the hotel, nearly running over a few spirit travelers.

Once she set the brakes, she jumped out and marched up the steps to the hotel. There had to be a room available because she couldn't stand to be around Richard. And after the kiss they had shared, the temptation would be too much.

She wandered the empty lobby and spotted Perry.

"Hello, Kate. Decide to go for a swim?"

"Yeah, so is there a room available yet?"

Perry smiled. "As a matter of fact, I was on my way to tell Richard I have a room set aside for him."

"Good, if you give me his room number and key, I'll be sure he gets it."

Perry handed her the key. "Here you are. Room seven. Have you finalized the party plans?"
"Yes, Richard will give you all of the details. I think it should be at Moonlight Cove, Victorian theme. And I'll get the music list to you for the band tomorrow." She turned to leave.

"Be here at two for your therapy and a radical acceptance group meeting after. Nick went to the cottage to let you know."

"Thanks, Perry."

On her walk to the cottage, she ran into Nick.

"Finally, the woman I'm always in search of has wandered to me."

"Ha, so Perry filled me in, thanks." She whirled past him in a hurry, not in the mood for any conversation.

Once inside, she wandered to the shower in a daze, changed, gathered Richard's clothes and jacket, then put them on the doorstep with the key. *Should keep him out*. She wandered inside in a daze, never feeling lonelier. Everywhere her eyes roamed had her wanting Richard. Maybe a walk would provide a distraction. She snatched the map off the kitchen table and headed to Moonlight Cove. After a walk through the forest and by a lake, she recognized the cave entrance to the cove on the map.

The entrance proved to be perfect for their Victorian theme. She walked toward the large opening, picturing large heavy drapes around the edges with sconces. Inside, her eyes harmonized to the narrow dark tunnel she was in then the cove came into view.

The sunlight streaming in through the holes in the rock ceiling allowed enough lighting. *Richard would like it*. She thought back to the party plans and how fun of a night it would be with all of the decorations and guests dressed in costume. He would really like the dress she would wear and hoped to be able to find.

Ugh, who cared what he liked, the two-timing jerk?

The moonlight would create the perfect evening ambiance for the dinner. She might even teach a few dances beforehand, which would fall into rhythm with the theme of the night.

She walked behind the waterfall and stepped onto the ledge and into an alcove with a bubbling spring. Clair and Jonathan crossed her mind. How long they were together? And what started their romance? Did they disagree at times like her and Richard? And how could the author not finish the story? Why was she thinking of two people who didn't even exist?

She sat for nearly an hour, stewing and contemplating. Why hadn't he told her about his fiancée?

"I didn't mind the long walk at all, thanks." He stepped down from the ledge.

Speak of the devil. "How did you find me?"

"I know you. Not sure how, but I do."

"I left your things with your room key on the porch." When she went to leave, he blocked the path.

"I got them. I understand you're upset, but I would like you to hear my side of things."

"No." She stepped up on the ledge and into the open area of the cove. "I told Perry you'd give him the details of the party. We're done."

He placed his hands on her shoulders. "Under the circumstances, I shouldn't want you. I know. But I do."

"I shouldn't want you, either, and I can't, not now. It's not like any of this matters."

"What do you mean?"

"When we wake up, this will all be forgotten. You, this place, everything. Best we cut our losses now."

"You don't mean it, and deep down, I'll remember you, I'm certain of it, love." He caressed her face in his warm hands. "Last night, I heard your thoughts before we went to sleep and wanted you in my arms. If it weren't for the minor technicality of my fiancée, I would be able to act on my feelings for you. There's no need to cut anything off between us because I know right from wrong and so do you. I'm more than content being in the same room with you."

Lost in his eyes, her resolved weakened. There was no reason they couldn't be friends and enjoy what time they had while they had it. The present moment mattered most. So, she wouldn't think of their nonexistent future. She would be content with whatever time she had with him, however brief it might be.

"Richard, I think we should—"

"Richard!" Charlotte ran in the cave with Ashlee behind her. "We need you to come with us. Divine Intervention has an opening now. Will's more determined than ever to get Branson and has Russell helping him again."

He moved his hands from Kate's face. "Russell? What do you mean again? Why would he be involved? He's a doctor, not a spy. And didn't Will wake up?"

"Who's Russell?" She didn't recall him being mentioned when Ashlee and Charlotte came to discuss Will's revenge.

"Russell is my dad's best mate," he muttered. "But I don't understand why Will would call Russell." His gaze stopped on Charlotte.

"Russell helped Will and me stay incognito," Ashlee said. "He's been helping Will track Branson. He came often and helped with Madelyn's birth. Will trusts him."

His eyes narrowed. "Russell knows about you? Madelyn? All this time he knew and never told us?"

Charlotte clasped Richard's arm. "He's Will's godfather and is watching out for him. Russell has resources Will doesn't."

"What the bloody hell kind of resources?" His jaw

tightened.

"You remember when Russell worked with the police to find the man who killed his wife and daughter?" Charlotte said.

He nodded. "Vaguely."

"It wasn't only the police. He has connections with Interpol and rogue and retired agents. Russell has a thing for seeing that bad guys get what they deserve." Charlotte frowned at Kate. "I'm sorry we interrupted you two. Ashlee and I will wait outside."

When Ashlee and Charlotte were gone, she sighed. "You'd better go."

"When I'm done with the Divine Intervention business, I'd like to come to the cottage, talk with you some more."

She wanted nothing more. "It's better if you don't." She turned away from him.

"I don't understand."

Avoiding eye contact with him was best, she didn't think she would have the self-control to not kiss him again, give in and become an almost marriage wrecker. The ache to be in his arms made her heart break into what felt like razor-sharp pieces of glass because he belonged to another woman, and if she entertained him at their cottage, she would be too weak to only be friends.

"Being alone with you isn't a good idea, not after what happened on the beach." She could still feel his hands lingering all over her body. "Good luck with Will."

She bolted out of the cave without a backward glance.

Chapter Six
Early Return Granted

"You told her about Amber, then," Charlotte inquired while they sat in the hall on a bench and waited to see someone about Will.

He clenched his jaw. "What I could. She turned to fire before I could explain."

"Can you blame her?"

"No, but I don't love Amber. I thought I did, but my feelings for Kate make it all the more obvious. I'd like to talk things out with her."

"Make it fast. Once divine intervention makes a decision, you'll return like Will, unprompted exodus."

He frowned.

"Are you in love with Kate?"

"When did it happen?"

Charlotte laughed and hugged him.

Ashlee walked up to them. "Chester will see you now. Thank you, Richard."

"Don't thank me yet." He stood and followed Ashlee to a small office.

"He'll be right with you. Charlotte and I will wait for you outside." Ashlee shut the door.

He paced the room, wanting to get this mess with Will straightened out so he could get to Kate before he woke up. The thought of not remembering her made his head ache. He couldn't forget her though, could he? Not deep down. She was far too engrained in every one of his senses. He'd straighten things out with her; he had to because she belonged with him. He wanted all of her, vinegar and cupcakes. Not a likely combination, but she suited him.

A short, heavyset man walked in and shut the door behind him. "I'm Chester." He shook Richard's hand before he sat at the desk in the small room.

Chester scoured the paperwork. "We have discussed your case and, for your niece's sake, Madelyn, will send you to your body a week early."

"I was going to be here another week?"

Chester nodded. "Haven't you seen your medical records?"

He sighed. "Afraid not."

"This is a big mess you're volunteering to get into for Will. And if Kate lives, she may not for very long after she bumps into you."

He leaned forward. "What do you mean *if she lives*?"

"Her injuries are life-altering. She'll never dance professionally again. Deep down, she knows it and would rather die than not dance on a professional level, which is why she's skipping out on therapy and not accepting her predicament. And if she recovers and gets in Branson's path, he might…kill her."

His heart nearly stopped. "I'd like to see her chart."

"Normally, I wouldn't, but you are a doctor and statistics say there's a good probability you are supposed to be her protector. High enough odds, I'm guessing it comes all the way from the top." Chester handed him a folder.

He scanned her chart. While her injuries were most dreadful, he'd seen people worse off pull through.

He handed the chart to Chester. "Do you have mine?"

Chester shuffled and moved folders around on top of the desk. "Here you are."

He raked his eyes over the chart. It was a sobering feeling to see his life-threatening injuries spelled out on paper. "Thanks, explains a lot."

"We have much to do in the next twenty-four hours. Statistics will show you some scenarios with Kate so you are instinctive in wanting to protect her.

They'll also show you what they can of Will's possible future if he doesn't stop his revenge and one if he does stop."

"What about the party her and I are supposed to be hosting tomorrow evening? Will I leave before then?"

Chester shrugged. "Not sure. Would you like to stay for it?"

"Yes."

"I'll see what I can do." Chester stood. "Get some rest at the hotel after Ashlee briefs you on some things, and tomorrow morning, after breakfast, I'll take you to statistics for some scenario watching. You won't be able to help with the party but showing up for it shouldn't be a problem."

"Scenario watching." He followed Chester out of the room.

"Yes, and I must warn you it's going to be hard to watch. Scenarios are quite graphic. See you at ten tomorrow in the hotel lobby." Chester left him standing in the empty hallway.

He had to get to Kate and explain things to her.

"What did he say?" Ashlee asked.

"I'm waking up early. I need to see Kate."

"You'll see her later. I need you to come with us. Since early out has been decided for you, Ashlee has to brief you on some things, and there's someone that I want you to meet." Charlotte smiled.

He sighed. "Can't it wait? I really need to see her." Remembering the way Will had departed gave him a sick stomach. Disappearing in a flash seemed most unnatural, and he wanted to say goodbye tonight in case he didn't make it to the party.

"No, it can't." Charlotte pouted. "I want you to meet my husband."

"What?" He couldn't have heard her right.

"My husband, Henry, come on."

He shook his head. "What is it with you and Will and secret spouses?" He followed Charlotte and Ashlee out, guilt-ridden at Kate never dancing again and tense in anticipation of what graphic scenarios he'd be exposed to the next day.

***

She ditched both her therapy appointment and radical acceptance rah-rah meeting. Hiding out from Nick resembled avoiding the F.B.I. He seemed to be everywhere she turned. When he found her in the women's health section of the library, she faked cramps and retreated to the cottage.

But thoughts about her dad consumed her. She had considered the therapy deal after her dad died. After all, seven years of living on a life or death roller coaster about his imminent death had taken its toll. Talking to a stranger about her problems would only be a waste of time though, wouldn't it? And no counselor could change what had happened to her dad: his misdiagnosis and cover-up by the doctor they'd trusted to treat him. When she recalled the lawsuit and trial her family went through once they learned the truth, a chill ran up her spine.

And when the panic attacks started, only her denial had her having MSG poisoning or some heart ailment or murmur the doctors must have neglected. How could she have panic attacks? She was an accomplished ballerina and had everything under control. She laughed at herself, because crying didn't suit her, and opted for tea.

It brought to mind what Richard said last night. How, after a good cry, she'd feel better. If only she could cry buckets and be done. But anger filled the place of sorrow inside her and had grown old to revert to.

Suffocation by irritation needed to stop. Trying to find anything positive in her tart mood proved a challenge. On the upside, it had helped drive her to become the professional dancer she'd always dreamed of. But in the pit of her stomach, she didn't think her dancing status would ever be the same. No, she willed the thought away, wasn't an option.

And why had she only seen her dad for the briefest moment in the waiting tunnel? Richard had seen Charlotte twice now. Yes, they had some dangerous family business with his brother to deal with, but now with some time alone, missing her dad had filled the empty space around her to suffocation. She rubbed the center of her chest where the tight bubble always ached when she didn't cry.

If she cried it all out, she longed for Dr. Bennett's shoulder to brace her. She crinkled her nose. Why did her thoughts always come to him? Wouldn't he tell her to refer to the Hereafter packet and learn something she would already know if she'd read it? But she couldn't read it because then it would be difficult to deny the whole spirit-travel deal. After she added honey to the lemon tea, she snatched the packet off the table and started flipping through it.

The loud knock at the door made her jump and she spilled her tea down the front of her dress. The first tear fell. She wiped it from her cheek with the palm of her hand and tried to ignore the incessant knocking. When it didn't end, she pulled the door open, ready to give Nick a piece of her mind. But Richard stood before her.

"I told you not to come." She moved to shut the door.

He motioned toward her. "You wanted me here, so I came." He shut the door.

She swiped the hand towel off the table. "What do you mean I wanted you here?" She rubbed with a vengeance over her dress.

He stopped her by offering his hand. "I'm here only to lend my shoulder, if you'll have it."

She kept her head tilted down because of the onslaught of warm tears streaming down her face and let out a shaky breath. "How did you know?"

He put his arm around her and led her to the couch. "Do you really have to ask?"

She shook her head after they sat. He knew her so well, and, for the first time, she surrendered to it.

"I'm not going anywhere, Ms. Adams."

She dropped her face in her hands.

When he gathered her in his arms, she shattered there. Years of pent-up grief and frustration broke. He soothed her in silence and healed the wounded parts of her only he could. And when he handed her tissue and the breakdown subsided, it left her exhausted.

She nestled against his strong chest and closed her eyes. "Thank you."

He kissed the top of her head and stroked her hair. "You're welcome."

She listened to his steady heartbeat, and eventually lulled into a peaceful sleep.

Chapter Seven
Picture This

Richard waited in a bright room smelling of fresh popcorn to view scenarios. It reminded him of a theatre. He sat on the lone chair in the middle of the bright and plush space, waiting for the show to begin. Ashlee and Charlotte had both explained it would be like watching a play.

After Kate left him alone in the cave, he'd met his sister's Scottish husband Henry, who happened to be a few hundred years older than Charlotte. Talk about mind-boggling. Henry had died at nineteen. He hadn't slept much thinking about it. But the real reason he hadn't slept at all was that holding Kate in his arms last night had him wanting to enjoy every last moment he had left with her. He had considered swinging by the cottage to say a proper goodbye but recognized she needed time to process him showing up there because of mind reading again. He'd left her most regretfully and before sunrise. She would need time to accept herself allowing him to comfort her during her much-needed cry.

He'd seen her after breakfast from across the room. Her avoidance kept him at bay. And he had to sign some paperwork in Divine Intervention which required his attention longer than he had liked. So now, he sat alone in the scenario room after two in the afternoon. Chester had mentioned he would get Richard's suit for the party while he watched.

"Are you ready, Dr. Bennett?" a soft female voice asked.

"No, but carry on," he said to the invisible figure.

"We'll start first with the good news, the one and only scenario happening if Will listens to you."

"Fat chance," he mumbled. Will's name should be

Hardheaded but he managed to hold on to a small speck of hope.

"It will seem as if the people in the scenario are in the room with you. Please remember they're only images."

The room darkened, except for the area in front of him where a spotlight shined down on what appeared to be Will and his baby girl. If Richard hadn't known better, he would have sworn he occupied the room with his brother and niece. She was precious.

Will held her in his arms and kissed her cheek before laying her in the cot. Will left the room and strolled to his front room where their parents sat. Will and his parents getting along made him grin.

The scene before him faded and another took its place. "Please say you'll think about it." Veronica Bennett, his mum, motioned for Will's hand. "You need a woman in your life."

"I have you and Maddie, Mum. I'm fine."

"Stop bothering the boy," Simon Bennett chimed in. "Will's never had trouble finding a date."

Will smiled. "What's her name?"

"Judy told me her name…Kay?" Veronica frowned.

"Kate, the woman's name is Kate Adams," Simon added.

"How do you know Judy?" Will asked.

"From Miles, he's one of your father's new business partners. She's helping Judy open a dance studio. Come on, William, come to dinner tomorrow night."

Will smirked at his father. "She won't stop asking questions or setting up blind dates if I don't, will she?"

Simon frowned. "Afraid not."

"Fine, dinner."

The scene faded.

Richard shook his head. No way in hell she would ever end up with Will.

"Is something wrong, Dr. Bennett?" the voice asked after the scenario disappeared.

"I'm fine. Please, go on."

"Right away. The next scenario involves both your brother and Kate Adams, and I do caution you, it is violent," the voice warned.

He inhaled a deep breath and let it out when the spotlight in front of him showed her and him sitting in a restaurant. He quite liked how they appeared together and the smile she gave him from across the dinner table. This was more like it. No more Will with Kate scenarios. He settled on watching the rest of the predicament.

Kate leaned into the table. "How long before Will notices us?"

"Shouldn't take long. He won't be too keen on us being here when he does. Here he comes. Hey, mate," he greeted Will, who stood beside their table.

"Leave," Will uttered through his teeth.

"You still have awful manners, Will." He stood. "Apologize to the lady."

"Get out of here," Will snarled.

She shot up. "Why don't we keep it down. And I don't want to leave, Will. I'm hungry."

"Go somewhere else, then."

Richard and Will continued to argue. She rolled her eyes and fled to the bathroom.

Watching the scene gave him the advantage of a larger perspective. He noticed a man, who had to be Branson, across the room while the scenario version of himself argued with Will. Branson walked down the hall leading to the loo and the scenario shifted with him, almost like a camera following the action in a film.

Branson waited for her to come out then stopped her. "You almost had me fooled." His Texas drawl, deep and dark, rumbled with malice.

She looked up at him. "Can I help you?" She tried to pull her arm from the grip Branson had on her.

"I thought you were someone I used to know, but she would have tried to kick me across the room. You didn't even blink when our eyes met. Come with me, darlin', whoever you are." He covered her mouth and held a knife to her throat. "You got it?"

In the viewing room, Richard tensed, the blood pounding in his ears. He'd always been the peacemaker in his family and avoided violence, but right now, more than anything, he wanted to kill Branson.

"It's not real, Dr. Bennett, a scenario for now. But likely at 99 percent," the voice announced.

He mentally urged the version of himself wasting time arguing with Will to move, get to Kate.

Branson rushed her out through the kitchen, his knife to her side. The few cooks preparing food were too busy to notice them.

She struggled until Branson sliced her across her forearm and dragged her out the door, his hand over her mouth to muffle her scream.

Richard's hands fisted into rage-filled bombs while he watched her fight tooth and nail.

No matter how hard she struggled, she couldn't get loose from Branson. The jerk grabbed her by her throat and lifted her off the ground.

He rushed to his feet. "Where the hell am I? Still arguing with Will? When do I show up?" Richard demanded of the voice.

She didn't answer.

Kate turned purple then gasped for air when Branson threw her to the dirt like a rag doll.

Branson kicked her in the ribs and lifted her to her feet before she spit in his face.

Richard admired her courage but feared the consequence. Even knowing the situation was a probability and may indeed never happen, he still sickened at the thought of her being attacked. Adrenaline surged through him, leaving him shaking and furious at the impossibility of reaching out and pounding Branson to a bloody pulp.

Branson backhanded her, and when she hit the ground, he lifted her by her throat off the ground.

"No!" His shout echoed in the empty viewing room.

He watched in relief and confusion as the scenario of him finally arriving and brandishing a pistol. *Why would I have a gun?* He shot at Branson who then released her from the choke hold and ran around the corner.

He knelt next to her and assessed her.

She held a hand on her ribs and the other over the blood dripping from her arm.

"Sorry, I know that hurts." He slid his jacket off and put it under her head before gently easing her back.

He scowled at the imprint of Branson's hand already forming into a bruise on her neck. Her eyes were dilated, and she looked cool to the touch. He recognized those symptoms as well as her pale skin and presumed rapid pulse that pointed to shock.

"Enough!" Richard shouted, and the room filled with light.

He'd never wanted to kill anyone, ever. Branson now held the number one spot on his hit list. He dropped to the chair, his hands still fisted.

"I did warn you," the voice echoed.

"What other scenarios are there?" He couldn't take any more like this.

"Many of the same. You get the idea. We need you to get the first scenario to come true."

"My brother isn't getting the woman I love."

"All right, but don't say I didn't warn you." The

room dimmed again.

Will, bloody and banged up from a gun fight. Kate and Richard were with him, bruised and beaten up, too.

Will was dying.

"This can't happen. My parents can't lose another child." He laid his palms to his forehead.

"This is the scenario where you and Kate are together; however, you lose your brother. There are four other scenarios where you and she are happily ever after, but Will still dies," the voice reminded.

"There has to be another way." He paced the room. "I'll figure out another way."

"Sorry. You don't have the power. What are you proposing?"

"I could go to her in New York, after Will or I kill Branson. I go for a medical convention or something then she won't be in danger. I run into her there, somehow, and we have the déjà vu thing happen."

"You don't take lives, Doctor, you save them."

"True, but Branson shouldn't get to live."

"You'll have to tell her to stay away from you or that you don't love her. Otherwise, the draw to be near you will be too powerful for the universe to stop. Even if you tell her those things, you are the reason she will live if she does. You're the only requirement she's chosen to fulfill since she's been here. I mean the party-planning assignment. And you also have to remember Will's choices have already put things in motion. I'm happy to discuss your ideas, but the likelihood of them occurring is slim to none. Statistics only project the likeliest of scenarios."

He paced some more. He wouldn't tell her he didn't love her, it was far too obvious he did, in fact, love her and he would not lie or mislead her. *Will cannot die. He has a daughter to tend to and he can't have the woman he loves. No way is he getting her.*

"Has the dinner party started?" he asked.

"It's beginning."

"I need to get there, but first, I need to talk to my sister."

He charged out the door and bumped into Chester.

"In a hurry to get to the party, I see. Here." Chester handed him the Victorian-era suit.

"You don't have much time," he called after him when he dashed out of the building and toward Charlotte's place. He had to hurry, and, maybe, if his sister did some meddling, Will would live and he would still get the chance to be with Kate.

Chapter Eight
Searing Light

"A little higher." Kate waved her hand to Nick when he lifted the swag of golden velvet cloth over the entrance to the cave. "There."

After she lit the last lantern, brightening up the entrance to the cave, she observed the work, pleased with how perfect it had all come together. The dinner party had started, but she hadn't seen Richard all day, not since breakfast, and, at the time, she hadn't been ready to talk to him. Not after breaking down like she had. It was not embarrassment by the nervous breakdown she had, not at all. Having him and his shoulder to lean on was much appreciated but he had already left when she woke up...why? She somehow felt betrayed by his absence and overwhelmed by how much she needed him. The business with Divine Intervention must have been successful. Did he return to his body? Her stomach lurched, but she pushed the thought away.

Nick fastened the material then stood by her. "Very nice. You and Richard did a superb job on the plans. And I like this dress much better. The one you showed up in, not you at all."

"Thanks. I like this one better, too." She brushed her hands over the ruby satin theatre dress trimmed with cream lace. She lifted the princess train and wondered when her mind-reading hunk would arrive. She'd be sure to be busy or pretend to be otherwise occupied when he walked in. She needed to see him, know he still existed in the Hereafter.

She followed Nick inside, and once they made it through the sconce-lit tunnel and out in the cove, she admired the beauty their day of hard work had manifested. The moonlight illuminated like a chandelier for the dance area, and the tables were draped lavishly with bright colors and fine fixtures.

"You're stunning." Perry kissed her hand. "Richard must be running late, but he'd better show up soon. You two *are* the hosts."

She frowned at Perry and scanned the moonlit cove. *Where are you, Dr. Bennett?* She went to the left of the tunnel where she could see guests arrive and watch for him. She twirled the loose curls below her shoulders in her fingers then shifted the barrette fastened loosely in her hair. She wandered the room in torturous anticipation. More than anything, she wanted to see him.

But instead of Richard, her dad stepped in front of her.

"Katie, you're... Wow." Her dad gave her a slight grin. "A lot like your mom."

She started to tremble. "You're really here. I'm not dreaming."

What did one say to their dead father? Apparently, not much. All she could do was fall into his arms when the dam inside her broke all over again. Hadn't she shed all of her tears last night?

"Guess you're not holding up as good as I thought." He led her to a corner where they could have some privacy.

She sobbed and tried to breathe, but it hurt, so she held on to her dad for dear life and soaked the shoulder of his white button-up shirt.

"I know." Her dad rubbed her arm then squeezed her tighter. "I've missed you, too."

"This is all too much," she whispered before she hiccupped. And she didn't want to blubber with what little time she'd get to spend with her dad. "I thought about being able to see you again and what I'd say." She bit her lip when it trembled. "I didn't think I'd cry like this."

"You need to cry. Holding all of it in only makes it worse. I'm okay, cancer-free. Has to make you feel better." He grinned at her.

"It does, I..." She sighed. "You've missed so much, and I miss you being there."

"I've been there. I saw you dance before Christmas in New York then saw you all at your sister's birthday party. I come to what I can; you just can't see me." He frowned. "Lyza's wedding, the father-daughter dance, it tore me up, too, Big K. I haven't seen you tear out of a place since the time you thought you saw an octopus in Lake Mead."

She laughed. It felt good to remember how she had jumped off her dad's back and jetted through the water to the shore. "I was eight."

He laughed. "Fun to watch. Made me think of switching you from ballet to track. It's good to see you smile."

"You, too." She let out a long sigh of relief, the pain bubble in her chest and throat were gone. The joy hit her like sunrays all over her skin.

"I don't have much time." He wiped her eyes and smiled at her. "I know it's not the father-daughter dance, but it's close enough." He held out his arm and led her to the dance area under the starlight filling the room.

"I don't want to wake up," she admitted.

"What?"

"Mom's a mess. Kara and I are too far away to help her, and even if we were there, she'd pretend she was okay. I don't want to forget any of this time here, and seeing you...if I stay here, I'll remember. And what if I can't dance again? I can dance here."

He twirled her around then held her close. "Your mom will be fine. And what if you start a new life, new plan?"

She shook her head. "I don't want a new life. I

liked the old one."

"Sure, maybe to a fault though."

"What do you mean?"

He grinned. "You've accomplished one dream. What about the other dream you had to have a husband and family? You've been distracted and so focused on your dance career, you forgot the importance of love and relationships. This accident and the time you've spent here is a gift, Katie. It's a chance to reevaluate and maybe even get both of your dreams to come true."

Tears welled up in her eyes as she listened to her dad and, along with them, a desire to have what her dad spoke about. She didn't want a family with anybody. She wanted to share a life with Richard. What an idiot she'd been, wasting all day because of her immature reaction to his confession. When she gazed around the room and didn't see him, a jolt of panic gripped her insides. What if she had come to her senses too late?

Her dad grinned. "He's on his way."

"You know about him? I want you to meet him."

"There isn't time, but I approve. Big K, I came to tell you to fight to live. Whatever your life will be, I want you to fight for it. You have so much you've already accomplished in twenty-four years. See what you can do the next fifty or sixty." He put his arm around her and walked her to the side of the dance floor.

She sighed. "You're leaving."

The memory of their last goodbye, like a bad dream. Her dad telling her he hadn't expected her to talk at his funeral as he'd known it would be too hard for her. This parting, still bittersweet, didn't have any of the dread and sorrow of their last separation.

"For now. I'm always with you, Kate. And let me leave you with this last bit of advice." He grinned.

"Stop trying to control everything. When you wake up, your life will be different than what you had in mind, but maybe different is better." He tugged gently on her ear like he used to when she was a little girl, his *I love you*.

When she blinked, he'd vanished. She wiped the tear on her cheek. "I love you, too, Dad."

She stood a pillar of grace, composure and poise on the outside, but inside, she had lost her dad all over again.

One last time, she swept the room for Richard.

***

In Richard's mind, Kate repeated his name like a mantra. The wounded tone of her voice summoned him from Charlotte's house.

He straightened his suit tie. "I have to go. Remember what we talked about. Meddle as much as you like, Charlotte, and do whatever it takes on this end of things to help me keep Will alive and remember Kate." He kissed his sister's cheek and started for Moonlight Cove, willing himself to stay present long enough to explain what she would allow him to.

When he made it to the cave entrance, he bent over to catch his breath for a moment. Her plea for him not to be gone still ringing in his mind, he stumbled inside.

Then he saw her standing alone by the pastry table. He was grateful for hearing her thoughts because, by the straight posture and the way she carried herself, he would never know she gave him any thought at all.

He stepped beside her. "I'm here."

***

Inside, she smiled a thousand times. "You're late."

"You're sad." He wore a worried expression.

She drank in the sight of how handsome he was in the velvet-trimmed charcoal frock coat. "Said goodbye to my dad."

"I'm sorry but delighted you were able to visit with him." He fiddled with the red satin ascot underneath his coat. "Goodbyes are never easy." He tugged at his collar.

"Let me."

"You're not going to strangle me, are you?" he teased.

"I should." She gripped the tie and slowly loosened it before she straightened his coat collar. Her hand lingered there.

"Thank you." His eyes narrowed at her.

"Is something wrong with my dress?"

"No, why do you ask?"

She pulled her hand from his collar. "You keep frowning at it."

He slipped his arm around her. "You are the most beautiful woman I've ever seen."

"Thank you, but don't compliment me."

"Why not?"

"You know why not."

He placed his hand on the small of her back. "Dance with me?"

"We shouldn't." She wanted to but thought about his fiancée.

His unhappy expression pressed her to verbalize.

"It's not that I don't want to dance with you." She clasped his hand, remembering she had decided to take advantage of every moment they had left together.

"Then say yes." He gave her an adoring stare.

After a split second, she agreed. When he led her onto the dance floor, the music stopped and a new song began. He embraced her in his strong hold. Being in the arms of the man she loved stung with sweet torture. She was wrapped in his eyes when the words to the song started.

The lyrics weren't familiar, but the melody echoed through her. The old Beatles song "Here, There and Everywhere" filled her with tenderness as the words held an exceptional meaning.

She narrowed her eyes. "I didn't put this song on the list I gave to Perry."

He pulled her close. "I did."

"Richard—"

He brought his finger to her lips. "I can't leave without attempting something to spark a memory of you. To somehow take with me, I mean. I play this song time and again on the guitar. Every word describes how I feel about you. Maybe it's why I've always fancied it. I may not remember this precise moment, but I hope to sense this, holding you."

His words brought stinging tears to her eyes. "You play the guitar?" She wished she'd get to listen to him strum to her someday.

He brushed his knuckles over her cheek. "I'll wish the same."

She gave him a defiant stare.

"Sorry." He winked.

She grinned. "I still don't like you hearing my thoughts, but I'm getting used to it." She'd let him read her every thought if he could stay. "I thought you said you couldn't dance?"

"I wanted an excuse to dance with you. Come with me." He caressed her hand and escorted her to the ledge behind the waterfall.

Her excitement in being with him was like before a performance, she could feel her pulse in every nerve ending, and the beautiful fear of being vulnerable to him had her knees trembling. The words to the song lingered deep inside her and kept her heart arrhythmic.

They stood by the hot spring, and steam rose from

the water.

"I don't think I have much time." He paced in front of her. "I heard you calling my name in your thoughts. I came to say goodbye."

She toyed with the jeweled necklace she wore. "I thought you'd already left."

"Not yet, but I guarantee it's soon. I can feel it somehow." He faced her. "I saw your medical records."

"Why would you see my records?"

"To assess the injuries you sustained. You have an epidural hematoma and some broken bones."

"An epidural what? And what do you mean assess?"

"Sorry. Blood between the skull and brain. Listen to me, love, I care about you and may need to protect you. Emergency surgery was performed and thus explains the coma." He embraced her. "My situation is similar. My spleen ruptured and was removed and there's severe blood loss which required twelve units of PRBCs—"

"PRB what?"

He narrowed his eyes. "Sorry, blood."

"Go on."

"I have a grade-3 concussion and plenty of broken bones. Kate, I'm concerned."

"You're concerned I won't make it?" Her dance career on earth had ended for sure. She'd be dancing for the angels now.

"No. I'm concerned about what will happen when you do. I saw a scenario where Branson gets to you."

"A scenario? What do you mean?"

"A glimpse of a possible future, depending on our actions and choices. I spent the afternoon being briefed, so to speak, to be better prepared to help guide events for the best possible outcome when I wake up. You have to promise me one thing. If Judy asks you to visit her, don't."

"I can't promise." She sensed she would know somehow. Her instincts would guide her to him.

"It was dreadful. I understand now why Will wants to kill Branson. I'll remember you and come to New York. Charlotte will do some meddling to assure I do."

"Branson kills me?" She swallowed a knot in her throat.

"No. I stopped him in the scenario. Not before he hurt you though. Please stay home, I'll find you. Do you trust me?"

Too soon to trust him? She did. "Yes."

"Thank you. Now, I have one more request. May I explain what you wouldn't let me the other day?"

She rested a hand on her hip.

"I went to Vegas, following after Will, although it made a convenient excuse to delay breaking off the engagement. Amber and my family have been friends for years. It's complicated, but I'm not in love with her."

"You're sure?"

"Positive. My family has money, and it's hard to know who likes you for yourself or the status. Amber comes from a similar lifestyle, and we were sensible at the time. I'm sorry I didn't tell you. I never meant to keep it from you or deceive you." He stroked her cheek with the back of his hand. "I wasn't expecting to feel what I do for you."

"This, us, it's—"

"Impossible? Too soon? How can this even be happening when we're not in our bodies? It's all I've thought about, and I don't want to think anymore. It's the damnedest thing, Ms. Adams, but I can't remember not knowing you."

She dropped her head against his chest, breathing in the familiar sea-and-summer spiced scent of him. *Say it, tell him.* "I'm in love with you, Dr. Bennett," she whispered.

He cradled her face in his hands. "I loved you when I saw you in the god-awful dress."

She smiled.

"But I fell more in love with you every moment after." He brushed his lips over hers.

Soft. Firm. Soul binding.

She gripped onto him tighter, not ready to let him go, reveling in the untamed pleasure consuming them both.

His lips bruised hers in the wild excitement they found themselves spinning in.

"I'm not ready to leave you," he whispered, dropping kisses over her neck.

"Stay with me. Fight it," she pleaded when he brought his forehead to hers.

"Don't watch me disappear. Keep your eyes shut, love. I'll find you," he whispered before kissing her again.

She did as he'd instructed, closing her eyes and tightening her clasp on him before a searing surge of light severed through them; tugging, splitting then wrenching them apart.

She didn't have the courage to open her eyes. The stillness surrounding her without him overwhelmed her, and she trembled. "Richard?" A raspy whisper came out.

She swayed, shell-shocked without him. He was gone.

No. No. No.

Chapter Nine
Limbo Line

When she came out of the stupor, she hurried to the dinner party to find Nick.

She spotted Perry near the dance floor.

"He's gone." She held her hand over her stomach.

"He woke up. I'm sorry, Kate. I know you two were getting better acquainted. Do enjoy yourself. You worked hard on the plans for tonight and should be dancing." He directed her to the others gliding across the floor. She tried to be present in the moment but longed to be in Richard's arms.

Her heart sank to the ground while she attempted to engage in friendly banter with the other guests. It wasn't their fault the man she loved had woken up before her. But she blamed each and every one of them with their wide smiles and laughter. How could they be so happy while she suffocated in what-ifs?

She watched Nick absently when he accepted a note from a robed messenger.

How much longer would she be here? However long it was, it would be an eternity without Richard.

Nick came up beside her. "Did you get to say goodbye to him?"

She nodded.

Nick sighed. "There's something I need to tell you."

"Sorry, what did you say?"

"I have some grim news."

"I'm listening," she said.

"I need to take you to the Limbo line."

She gave him a *yeah right* glare. "I'm not really in the mood to party, and call me crazy, but a limbo line doesn't fit our theme."

"You misunderstand, Kate. As of now, your life's

in limbo. You're dying."

***

I'm dying.
Lightning struck and thunder boomed overhead.
She'd gone numb. The rain poured around them,
muddying the dirt road as they traveled by carriage
from the hotel to the Limbo line. Tiny pieces of her
heart tore away in small fragments. Not at the thought
of not going to earth to be the dancer she'd always
wanted to be, but because the thought of never seeing
Richard again seemed unbearable. Would she be
tortured to watch him live his life with another
woman? So unfair. Now, she knew what she wanted,
but it had been snatched from her forever.

"Adele will be your Limbo rep. You'll like her."
Nick stopped the carriage in front of a gold building
with crystal windows. Shadowy prisms danced toward
the starlight.

She gave Nick a desperate glance. "I'm not afraid
to die, Nick, but I'm not ready to."

He sighed. "I understand."

After they drifted inside the large double doors,
she waited in line with a few others then a redheaded
Adele greeted them.

"Good luck." Nick smiled at her before turning to
leave.

Adele put her arm around Kate's shoulder. "You'll
like your room."

She, in a state of shock or maybe detachment,
wanted to return to her body now—she was ready.
Dance career or not, getting reinstated to live her life,
whatever it turned out to be, mattered most.

"We're next, dear." Adele moved them forward.

When they were assigned a room, she moved into
an anesthetized state.

"There's a change of clothes for you in the closet then rest on the chaise lounge." Adele poured her a glass of water from a mint-green porcelain pitcher and handed it to her. "I'll check on you in a while."

She sipped the sweet water and changed into a buttercream gown. She lay on the lounge chair and became more disconnected. She closed her eyes and hoped she'd know her fate soon. She drifted off into a meditative sleep, still feeling conscious and aware of her predicament but resting deeply.

How long she'd been here she wasn't sure, but she thought she heard whispering voices around her. Her heavy lids fluttered open long enough to see Charlotte standing beside Perry before they closed and she slipped into a deep sleep.

***

"Rules, rules, and more rules. You saw them together. They're perfect for one another. There has to be something Divine Intervention can do to engage a memory reboot."

"Charlotte, you aren't even supposed to be here. And rules are in place for a reason."

"Come on, Perry." Charlotte glanced at Kate asleep in the lounge chair. "She has to return."

Perry sighed. "Still uncertain. The only requirement she fulfilled was planning the dinner party with Richard."

"Should count for something." Charlotte flipped through the pages of a small handbook. "I'll find a rule to fit this situation."

Perry wandered the room and paused in front of Kate. "She's borderline, the space between life and death is hardly separate now. She's young, but it won't save her from death if it's her time."

"Aha!" Charlotte held the book up to Perry. "Right here. Section two."

Perry browsed over the page and shrugged. "They

were getting close and definitely moving in the soul-mate direction, but even if she remembers him in her dreams, they have to meet in person and experience the déjà vu; otherwise, they won't feel the need to come together. Even if she lives and goes to New York, he's still in England."

Charlotte let out a long breath. "Minor technicalities. All I'm asking for is a chance to give them a life together if she makes it. And one requirement fulfilled is better than none."

Perry smiled. "Aren't you on probation? You'll only get moved farther down the angel list if you keep intervening in things you should leave alone. And Henry wouldn't approve."

"Leave Henry to me. The angel list can wait. This is important to me, Perry. You're the head of Divine Intervention and can give me the okay, so do it already." Charlotte grinned at him.

Perry walked to the door and stopped. "*If* she lives, I'll put you over it. But you have to make sure the connection to get them to meet is valid. Then there's the imminent danger she'll find herself in getting involved with Richard. It's concerning," he speculated. "No ghost appearances from you or meddling." Perry gritted his teeth.

Charlotte paced then bent down in front of her. "You have to want to live your life, even if it means a life you didn't plan," she whispered. "Want to live, I'll do the rest from here."

**

I'll do the rest from here. I'll do the rest from here. The tunnel she stood in opened like a portal into a hospital room, and she hesitated to take a step out. The light poured over her, warm and familiar, and now had her in no hurry to leave it. Inspecting the hospital room gave her a chill and confused her.

Unsure, she stepped out of the light and walked to her still and bandaged body. Did she want to stay here? The various tubes and beeping monitors around her didn't make her want to stay. Terrified, she shivered, her breath icy. She glanced over her shoulder; the tunnel still called to her. *You have to want to live your life.*

Did she? What life would she be going to? The light had been much warmer. When it started to fade, she moved toward it. Too late. The portal of light disappeared. Would she be stuck here? She sat by the body on the bed and studied what she could see of the face. Bruises and bandages couldn't hide what was undeniably her face. *You have to want to live your life. If you don't choose now, you'll be a ghost.*

Dr. Bennett, she loved him. What was his name? Her mind went blank. She only thought *him* and instinctively reached for the bruised body's hand.

Darkness enveloped her.

How do I go back to living when I feel so dead?

Chapter Ten
Déjà vu

Lusty Glaze, crowded as usual in June, had Richard sitting on the shore and strumming his guitar. Jack and Will would arrive at any moment. They were meeting him to play rugby on the beach.

He couldn't believe it had been six months since the accident. Being a surgeon was no longer the plan. His right hand had been crushed badly in the collision. He wiggled his stiff fingers and rubbed out the cramp in his palm. The scar had healed nicely, he thought while he studied it. At least he could still be an emergency room doctor.

His recovery had been long and tedious. The scars he had acquired on his arms from the road rash in the accident made him resemble a man who'd been wounded in battle. But it had given him a second chance at life, and he'd seized it immediately after waking from the coma, starting with ending his engagement to Amber.

Naturally hurt, confused, and angry at him, confirmed why he had avoided breaking it off in the first place. To spare her feelings instead of freeing them both from a big mistake.

But after he broke off the engagement, the heavy burden lifted, replaced with instant solace. And they both deserved to find their soul mates. He'd never really believed in it, one true love. But after the accident, his view shifted and he had a hunch he would find her, the woman in his dreams.

After the accident, he'd had reoccurring dreams and heard a woman's voice he knew somehow. Mad? Of course. He never saw her face, and she always had her back to him. Their environment always appeared hazy, almost like a watercolor painting faded by the sun. But deep down, he knew the place in time and recognized her voice.

"Come on, mate," Jack yelled from farther down the beach.

He stood and waved. While he walked toward him, Will scanned the beach; who was he looking for? He'd been following his brother for months now. Will was definitely up to no good. And now Richard seemed to be in the same boat. Carrying a handgun, a prosecutable criminal offense in the UK, became natural to him.

He kept one in his car, his home, and on his person at all times.

Prompted in dreams by his sister to have a weapon, it made no sense to abide them.

All she went on about was how Will was headed down a dangerous path and he needed to protect someone. Upon waking, he couldn't shake the dreams. They were as vivid as reality.

So, he enrolled in a few martial arts classes, figuring, why not? He'd been in a few fights as a young bloke, but in his nocturnal conversations with Charlotte, she assured him it may not be enough to help Will.

He approached his brothers, and they started their rugby game. *Yes, it might be time to call a psychologist.*

***

Something about Lusty Glaze mirrored another well-known beach. Like a cherished memory tucked away in the corner of her mind. Kate wrote her name in the sand with her finger while the sun faded into the sea. *Glad to see the crowds thin out.* She thought to how claustrophobic it had been during the music gig.

She'd been in Newquay for a week and still

wondered why she'd agreed to come. Something about traveling to England made her stomach drop and swarm with butterflies at the same time. Some unknown force wanted to warn her. Yep, she sounded ridiculous. Warn her about what?

When she arrived in England, she hadn't been surprised to feel so familiar and at home. She found herself searching the shore for a reunion with an important man. *Weird.*

Redirecting, she had nothing pressing in New York. Her professional dance career, now a thing of the past. She'd recovered nicely from the accident, according to her doctor, and could live an active life. But she'd sustained enough damage she'd never dance pointe again. Still trying to accept it but not having much luck.

When she'd bumped into her old dance teacher after she'd been axed from the ballet, she turned down her first offer to come to England and regroup. But Judy wouldn't stop checking on her when she came to New York or insisting she come see her in Cornwall. And now, she didn't want to be anywhere else.

Although, the recurrent dream she'd had her first week here weighed on her mind. She couldn't see the man in her dreams, but she could hear him, his voice both familiar and soothing to her.

Smooth as his English accent sounded, his message didn't feel right. *Don't come to England. Stay home*, he whispered from behind her in her dreams. Had she dreamt it before she left, it would have spooked her not to come, simply because it seemed uncannily real. But having the dream here made her feel like something she'd lost would be found. What though? She needed a new game plan, and maybe a better life begged her to find out what it might be.

Judy kept her busy in the first week. Not sightseeing or spending time at the beach but soul-searching and facing what she hadn't wanted to. Judy had known about her dad, and talking to her about him had helped. It was coming up on the eighth-month mark since his death.

Sure, she had her mom and sister to talk to, but sometimes getting an objective point of view helped her snap out of the sullen life she'd somehow shifted into living.

Judy had told Kate of her own losses and regrets. The main one seemed to haunt Judy, giving up her baby girl for adoption. She'd become pregnant before her boyfriend had been killed in a car accident and her career started to take off.

Dance became her life; nothing and no one else ever came before it, which left Judy lonely—until Miles came along last year and swept Judy off her feet. They ran a bed-and-breakfast, which had become a great summer job for Kate. Working had been her only condition in visiting them. She wouldn't come unless she earned her keep. She had some funds left in savings but didn't want to touch it. Now that she faced an uncertain future, the cash served as her only security.

Kate sighed, feeling cheated. She stood and brushed the sand off her bare legs before pulling a short yellow dress over her black bikini. She secured her shoulder-length hair back into a small ponytail. Wanting a change after the accident, she'd chopped it.

Glancing at her phone, she realized the time had come to meet Judy and Miles for dinner, so she gathered her chick-lit book, shook out her towel, and tossed them into a small bag before heading to a restaurant simply called The Restaurant. She stared at the ocean waves glowing in the fading sunlight, and she was soon lost in the deep swells rising towards the shore. What would she do with her life? Would it ever be as satisfying as dancing had been?

When she turned from the waves, someone tackled her to the ground, knocking the wind out of her. Flat on her back, she stared up and into the most wounded blue eyes she'd ever seen. Why did they seem familiar? Tall, dark, and handsome lifted himself up quickly and stared accusingly at her as if she'd run into him. She'd seen him somewhere, but before she could figure it out, he walked off. *So much for chivalry.*

"Are you daft, Will?" a smooth voice spoke. "I'm sorry about my brother. You all right?"

The guy who knocked her over had been attractive, but this man was breathtaking. She couldn't stop staring up at him. Yes, easy on the eyes and in rock-hard shape, but she had the strangest and loudest déjà vu ever, distracting her from her instant attraction to him. His voice was the one from her dreams...but how?

"Have we met?" he asked when Will walked away.

She shook her head.

"Can you speak?" He grinned.

She laughed. "Sorry. I'm still trying to breathe. Got here last week and this is the first time I've come to the beach."

"I'm Richard."

"Kate." When she accepted his extended hand and he lifted her to her feet, a flicker of memory teased familiarity in her mind.

"Where did Will run off to?" another ridiculously handsome man said after he ran up to them.

She searched the beach for photographers, thinking these men had to be in a photo shoot.

Richard shrugged.

"I'm Jack." He shook her hand. "Are you all right?"

"Yes, thanks." At least Richard and Jack had proper manners.

Jack gave her a sheepish grin. "Sorry, I'm

responsible for Will plowing you down. My throw he tried to catch. He's not very good at rugby though. I'll go find grumpy. Nice meeting you."

She bent over to pick up her phone and book that had fallen out of her bag when she was knocked over. Richard beat her to it and gathered her belongings and handed her the bag.

"Thanks."

"No worries. You're American?" He walked beside her toward The Restaurant.

"Yeah."

"Are you coming for Fat Face next week?"

She couldn't have heard him right. "What did you say?"

He smiled. "Fat Face Night Surf."

"I didn't know anything about it."

"You should come. I promise you my rude brother Will won't."

"Come on!" Jack yelled.

"I hope to see you there." He waved to Jack and moved away from her slowly. "And again, I'm sorry about my rude brother." He hesitated then jogged away.

Immediate distress had her eyes tearing up. Why? Sure, it was sad to see a hot guy get away, but this overwhelming tide of heartfelt emotion had to be worse than ridiculous.

She saw Judy off in the distance then come up beside her. "I see you've met Richard."

"Yeah. Where's Miles?"

"Letting us have some girl time. Come on, then, lovey. Let's get you some of the best fish and chips around."

***

She tossed and turned before finally falling asleep.

Richard showed up in her dream, and they stood in some decked-out lobby, and she remembered his leather jacket. She sported the hideous bridesmaid's dress from Lyza's wedding. They waited in line for something. Seeing her shiver, he slid his jacket over her shoulders. The moment seemed to linger.

She jolted awake, her heart racing. Why did she find him so familiar? She didn't have time to be boy crazy while trying to figure out her life, and she was a little too old for boy crazy thoughts.

But his voice had sounded like one she'd known for years. She fluffed her pillow and sighed before falling asleep.

Chapter Eleven
Fat Face

"Choreography would be good for you, or opening up a dance studio with me." Judy handed her a cup of tea and sat beside her on the couch in the living room.

She shrugged. "I don't know. I've thought of both but don't want to end up bitter. Showing others how to do what I can't anymore. I know"—she put her hands up when Judy raised her brow—"I'm feeling sorry for myself, but I'm thinking of something unrelated to dance."

"Don't go there. Showing others what you've done is rewarding, and seeing them succeed is delightful. Every time I saw my students dance, it thrilled me to see their hard work pay off."

"But you never lost your lead dancer status. I'm not the dancer I was." She sipped her tea.

Judy sighed. "No, you're not. But you have to use your talent, Kate. It's still there. You've wallowed long enough, dear. It's time to live your life. It may not feel like a second chance when you don't have the life you worked for, but you nearly died, and you're here for a reason. Don't waste time being bitter. Take it from me. I regret not keeping my baby, especially now I'm with Miles. But I'm going to enjoy having him to dote over and be a bit motherly to you while you're here." She winked. "So, are you going to Fat Face Night Surf, or do I have to drag you over there?"

She crinkled her. "Not really my thing."

"I'm sure Richard will be there."

"So?" She glanced over her nails and couldn't deny seeing him again would be enjoyable. She'd dreamt about him enough the last week to see plenty of him. Sort of unsettling, dreaming of someone she didn't know. Mostly because she did feel like she knew him.

"So, let's head out." Judy carried the cups to the kitchen.

She reluctantly followed her. "When's Miles coming back?" She grabbed her sweatshirt from the hook behind the door.

"Late tomorrow night. If we hurry, we'll see the fireworks." Judy draped a bright-green sweater around her shoulders and led the way.

Once they found a spot on the crowded beach and spread out a blanket, they watched the surfers compete.

She rubbed her hand over her charm bracelet as she always did when anxious. Why did she care if Richard showed up at the beach? Nerve wracked; she could not avoid searching the crowd for him.

"There's Jane Crouch, dear. I need to talk to her about the remodel for the B&B. Give me just a few minutes." Judy hurried through the spectators and embraced who had to be Jane, in a tight hug.

She wondered why Miles and Judy were remodeling, but they insisted it needed to be repainted and modernized. Kate preferred it the way it was.

"You decided to come." Richard grinned down at her, casually dressed in loose jeans and a T-shirt.

"I had to see what fat faces had to do with night surfing."

He laughed. "Mind if I sit?"

She nodded then he dropped down beside her.

"What do you think so far of night surfing?"

"What I can see is very impressive."

He nodded. "How are you enjoying England?"

"Very much. It's a little warmer than I thought it would be."

"You came at the right time." He smiled. "You sure you've never been here before? I know it sounds like a line of trash, but I'm sure I've seen you somewhere."

She knew the feeling. "Maybe I resemble someone

you know."

"No."

"Kate." Judy bent down beside them. "I'm going with Jane to go over some decorating ideas."

"I'd better go." She pushed to her feet, but Judy gently guided her down.

"Stay. Hello, Richard. How's your mum?" When he stood, she gave him a tight hug.

"She's great, thanks."

"Do see she gets to me safe, if you don't mind. Have fun." Judy gave her a conspiring grin.

"I really should go," Kate said.

"I agree with Judy. Stay." He sat down beside her. "You should see the fireworks anyhow."

Contentment came with sitting beside him, like they'd visited before. It was hard for her not to study him, his bright grin and clipped speech she could listen to all night. His voice rang as familiar as a companionship of years would.

How, she'd only met him? Listening to him evoked a familiar knowing and longing. It left her strangely drawn to him in a way she'd never been drawn to anyone before. After the fireworks, she shook out the blanket and tucked it under her arm.

"Not now," he mumbled under his breath when a tall, leggy brunette moved in front of Kate.

"Who's this?" The brunette planted her hands on her hips.

"Amber, this is Kate." His jaw tightened. "Amber and I have been friends for a long time."

"Friends?" Amber raked her eyes over her. "We were engaged," she spat at him.

Kate frowned.

"Good night, Amber." Richard snatched the blanket Kate had tucked under her arm. "Sorry, my car's over there." He pointed to a black Porsche.

"I can walk." Her gaze wandered to Amber who

still glared them both down.

"Enjoy his charm while it lasts, Kate!" Amber shouted.

"I'll walk you." Richard sighed. "It's been nearly six months since I broke it off with her. She's a bit stubborn."

She couldn't blame the woman for being upset. She'd been through difficult breakups of her own plus one broken engagement. And he seemed like the perfect catch.

"Breakups are tough."

"Yeah, you ever been engaged?"

"He left me and married my cousin. I was upset at first, but they belong together."

"You don't say." He raised a brow. "You're forgiving." He paused with a sigh. "Amber is obviously a grudge holder. You're also quite small. How tall are you?"

"Five four. And you're tall."

"I suppose."

They got to the B&B, and he stopped and inspected it. "Quaint, the changes they've made are taking shape."

Judy came through the front door. "There you are. Thank you for seeing her home. Come inside for some tea, won't you, Richard?" Judy pulled them in and pushed them onto the couch. "I'll be right back with some tea and cakes. Jane and I are going over paint samples in the kitchen." Talking a mile a minute, Judy hustled into the kitchen, not waiting to see if they wanted tea.

She shrugged. "Judy's excited to have someone to pay attention to. Her husband's away on business, and she swears I'm her long lost daughter. Plus the B&B is under a remodel, so she's going nuts not having people to cater to."

Richard tapped a finger on his knee. "How do you

know her?"

"She was my dance teacher at Julliard. I ran into her a few months ago, and she bugged me until I agreed to come for a visit."

"Julliard? Impressive. What type of dance?"

"Ballet." She didn't want to go into a long explanation, so she hurried and changed the subject. "What do you do?"

"I'm a doctor."

She cringed.

"I've never been frowned at for being a doctor."

Judy brought in some tea and cakes and hurried to the kitchen.

She handed him a cup.

"Thanks, but do tell me why me being a doctor brings a frown to your face."

"Did I frown?" There were good doctors out there. They weren't all unethical as she had experienced with her dad, but she couldn't imagine falling for anyone in the profession.

"Well?"

"Cake?" She offered him the plate full of desserts.

He reached for one and bit into it, not pressing her further.

"Why did you break off your engagement?" Nosy Kate alert.

He nearly choked and coughed.

"None of my business. Never mind."

He shook his head. "I realized I liked her but wasn't in love with her."

"Must have been hard for her to hear."

He set his cup on the coffee table. "The very reason why I'd put it off so long. Once I did it, a heavy weight lifted."

She studied the scar along his jaw. Why did even his scar seem familiar? "What happened?"

"Sailing trip at 19; rope hit me across the jaw and

sliced it."

"You go sailing often?"

"Not as often as I'd like but, yes, from time to time. Now, tell me why you dislike doctors?"

"It's a long story."

"Why don't we discuss it over dinner?"

"It's after nine."

"I meant tomorrow night."

She didn't want to make an excuse, but she shouldn't get involved with him.

"It's only dinner. You do eat, don't you?"

"Sometimes."

"Good, I'll pick you up tomorrow around six...be hungry." He stood and strode to the door. "Good night."

Then he was gone, the door clicking shut behind him.

She slowly sank into the couch. Oh yeah, she was falling for him all right.

***

He hadn't meant to leave in such an abrupt manner. He jogged to his car and paused before starting it up.

"What is it about Kate that seems so familiar?" He sighed.

He had wanted to visit and find out as much as he could about her, but didn't he already know her? Somehow? Someway? Her voice was the one from his dreams; he knew for certain.

Pulling onto the road, he chewed on his bottom lip. Why did the woman despise doctors? The answer, buried in a shallow grave at the edge of his thoughts, wouldn't rise.

"You're losing your mind, mate," he spoke to himself on the drive home, now more determined than ever to find out why his thoughts hinted already knowing her.

Chapter Twelve
Touch

"You've helped more than enough with the painting. Hurry up and get ready for your date," Judy shouted at her from across the dining room.

"It's just dinner. I won't be here long enough for it to be anything more." She stepped down from the ladder and wiped the back of her hand over an itch on her cheek. "Besides"—she pointed to the last wall waiting to be lathered with color—"I have an hour before he gets here." She nodded to the clock in the hall.

"Clock is an hour off. I really need to fix that."

"What?" She set the brush down and smeared paint from her hands over torn jeans.

"Judy?" Miles called from the front room, walking in a moment later with Richard in tow.

"Darling!" Judy jumped into Miles' arms. "You're early." She kissed him and glanced at Kate. "Richard says he's here to take our guest to dinner."

"You've got a grey spot there." He pointed and then wiped her cheek with his finger. He glanced around the room. "Nice work."

"Thanks, I'm sorry. Lost track of time." Her face flushed with heat from his presence and concern at her frumpy appearance being up since sunrise and no makeup or gown to greet his royal hotness. "Give me fifteen minutes." She hurried out of the dining room and up the stairs.

She undressed and showered in record time and managed to get all of the paint off her face and hands. She threw on a long sundress and slipped into some sandals. After she dried her hair, she dusted some blush across her cheeks and eyelids then shaded her lips with a berry colored gloss for the final touch.

She eyed her reflection and congratulated herself with getting ready in fourteen and a half minutes. Her hair was a little damp, but she gave it a light touch of hair spray and snatched her purse off the bed and pinched her nose. *It's just dinner.*

When she came downstairs, she found him and Miles chatting in the living room.

They stood when she walked in, and Judy came in behind her.

Richard glanced at his watch. "That was fast."

"Hope it's somewhere casual." She placed her hands on her hips.

"Italian all right?" He shoved his hair back away from his face.

"La Luna?" Miles asked.

"Of course," Richard said.

"Have fun." Judy hugged her. "And I want to hear all about it. I'll be waiting up," she whispered into her ear.

"Bye." She practically ran out the door.

"Have you been painting all day?" Richard opened the car door for her.

"Since sunrise."

He got in and started the engine.

"I want to help Judy with as much as I can before I leave. What did you do today?" She fastened her seat belt.

"Tried to kill time until I could see you."

Her pulse accelerated. "You didn't have to work?"

He shook his head. "The next three days I'll be at the hospital." He stared at her. "There's something so familiar about you, your eyes and voice particularly. But I'd know if we'd met before."

"Are you saying I'm unforgettable?"

"Yeah."

"The déjà vu is mutual. I've racked my brain trying to think if I may have seen you somewhere and can't remember where. It's like being stuck with the right word on the tip of your tongue, and you know it but you can't get it to come to the surface."

"Frustrating, isn't it?" He drew in a long breath, and she was pleased with how relaxed she felt around him. Not the typical first-date tension.

They made small talk about his brothers and family until they arrived at the restaurant.

While they waited for a table, she glanced around the brightly lit room and paintings on the walls.

Once they were seated across from each other and had ordered, he pulled the straw from the wrapper and bit down on it. "What do you do when you're not on holiday?"

She had to get used to her new reality, but it wasn't going to be tonight. "I'm switching careers."

She'd eventually figure out what she was going to do with the rest of her life and how she would come to terms with her lost dream, but, at the moment, the pain was still too raw to share with anyone else.

"Brilliant, so no more ballet?"

She rested her chin on her palm. "No."

"Too bad. You definitely look the part."

"The part?" She sipped her water.

"Fit, small, graceful, and you have the straightest posture I've ever seen."

"Thank you."

"And you're a natural beauty. Which I have to say is quite refreshing."

"As opposed to?"

"You know, the women who pile their faces so thick with the gunk, it's distracting; hard to get to know someone when they resemble a clown."

She tilted her head. "I've never been one for too much gunk. Although, I'm a big fan of foundation to cover up the freckles."

"I like your freckles. Glad you didn't cover them

up."

She played with her hair. "There wasn't time."

"Good."

Their salads came, and while they ate, they fit into a comfortable pattern of getting to know one another through their pasta and dessert.

"All right, time for you to tell me why you find doctors so wretched." He clutched his chest in an offended manner.

She laughed. "I never said that."

"Didn't have to. I saw your face contort the other night."

"It's a downer. And I'm having too good a time pretending you're not a doctor."

He raised a brow. "What exactly are you pretending I am?"

"Keep in mind that I only have the impression of what Hollywood has sold the American people on you Brits, so I'll start first with a professor."

He chuckled before folding his arms over his chest. "Hogwarts."

"Bingo."

He stroked his chin. "Go on."

"A spy."

"I hope you're picturing Bond and not Powers."

She pressed her hands to her cheeks. "Your teeth are far too straight to be Powers. Ever thought of going into either one of those careers?"

He narrowed his eyes. "An agent more than a professor with a wand, but I do enjoy being a doctor and would like to know why it's a problem for you."

When she tapped her fingers on the table, he extended a hand over hers, and their eyes locked.

His touch stirred a memory of something she knew she had never experienced, or had she? Time slowed. The dinner chatter hushed around them. Only aware of the memory flash her mind's eye showed her, she was sitting beside him in a tiny cottage. Their nestled proximity and the candlelit room made his bright-blue eyes soft and beckoning.

Shaken by the phantom recollection, she tried to tug her hand away, but he tightened his grip. Another flash of memory played out of him brushing her hair back as it fell loose from her braid.

"We should go." She jumped to her feet, dropped some money on the table, and sprinted outside.

He met up with her a few minutes later. She'd been pacing in front of his car.

He handed her the cash she'd left. "I asked you to dinner." He stuffed the money in her hand. "We need to talk." He opened her door.

She rubbed her hands over her eyes, still trying to get over the vision. Help, she found herself in dire need of a shrink. Hallucination? Or worse, maybe she had some latent brain damage from the accident the doctors had missed.

"How come when I touch you"—he fastened the seat belt—"it's like I already have?"

"I have the same question."

"You saw something, too?"

She exhaled. "Yeah, how did we see what appeared like a movie of us?"

He started the engine and rolled down the windows before pulling out of the parking lot.

Okay, time to change the subject from what transpired in the restaurant. "My dad was misdiagnosed." As sad as it made her to remember her dad's suffering, the vision thing happening with Richard? Way too intense to confront.

"You told me. I'm sorry. Cancer is a terrible illness."

Her mouth mirrored a cod fish. "What? I never told you." A panic attack threatening to emerge, she took several slow, deep breaths.

He shrugged. "You must have mentioned it at dinner. How else would I know your family went through a trial before you finished high school?"

She tensed her shoulders and rationalized maybe someone he knew had gone through something similar and this was a crazy coincidence.

"You said the doctors covered up their mistake."

"I don't know what's happening, but I never told you about my dad, and you shouldn't know I don't like hospitals or doctor's offices. Too many bad memories." Her thoughts drifted to the moans of patients heavily medicated from doses of chemical concoctions to extend their suffering, the pungent smell of death around her.

"I get it."

"I don't want any reminders of any of it. And I'm leaving in a few weeks. Not to mention this ESP of yours is freaking me out."

He pulled in front of Judy's then he leaned closer. "I'm freaked, too, and I'm not asking you to hang out in surgery or any doctor's office. I am asking you to spend more time with me so we can get to the bottom of this."

"You shouldn't know so much about me." She opened the door and rose from her seat and slammed the door. The weird déjà vu thing was making her heart race.

He came after her and, at the front door, he gently grasped her arms. "You're right. I shouldn't know so much about you. But the fact is I do, and I intend to figure out how. I'd prefer to figure it out together."

"This is crazy. Thanks for dinner." She reached to open the door, but he set his hand on hers, stopping her.

He stared at their interlocked fingers. "Even your hands seem familiar."

She couldn't move if she'd wanted to. His eyes

rose to meet hers, and the power behind his gaze sent her heart into an erratic pirouette.

She should run into Judy's and lock the door, escape while she could. Thoughts? She didn't have any. All she could do was enjoy the excitement he stirred inside her before another image of them reading letters in front of a fire sparked across her mind.

"I have to go." She pulled away.

He loomed closer and paused, his lips over hers. "Aren't you curious?"

She drew nearer. "Yes, but—"

He brushed his lips over her cheek and she closed her eyes. Her fingers gripped his hair, pulling him closer, and then his lips touched hers and in the heat of their passion, an image of them exploded inside her cozied up together in front of a fire in each other's arms.

He slowly parted his lips from hers. "Chemistry confirmed. I'm on call at the hospital the next three days. Then, we are going to figure this out."

"I'll be sightseeing."

He tucked a finger beneath her chin and tilted her face up. "Then I'll come with you."

Before she could say no, he pressed his lips to hers, imparting a short but tender kiss. "I'll see you soon, Kate."

He left her in a fog on the doorstep. A moment later he sped off. Judy opened the door and Kate faced her, a tornado of emotions rendering her thought process useless.

"Why are you home so soon?"

"I can't see him again."

Judy glanced at Miles sitting in front of the TV, oblivious to what was going on. "What?"

"I can't fall for him." She dragged her feet up the stairs.

"You already have."

Judy followed her into the bedroom, shutting the door behind her. She fell on the bed. "I'm leaving in a few weeks."

"Not if I have anything to say about it. And why are you in such a hurry to leave?"

"I have to figure out what to do. I can't stay here with you and Miles forever. I have to make a living, Judy."

Judy sat beside her and put her arm around her. "You will figure things out. But stay long enough to find out if it's something here." She gave her a tight squeeze. "I'll see you at breakfast."

Kate didn't sleep after she changed into sweats and turned off the light. Every molecule in her body hummed with the mystery of it all. Why did she dream of Richard? Why did touching him feel like coming home?

Maybe she now would be known as Crazy Kate. But he had seen something, too. Maybe they were going out of their minds together...

Chapter Thirteen
Breathe

"I thought you had to work?" She stood and brushed sand off her legs. She'd come to Lusty Glaze to relax, enjoy the sunset, and consider Judy's offer of going into a dance business together. Richard had been the last person she'd expected to see on the beach, but it made her smile.

He shrugged. "I stayed until someone could cover my shift. We really need to talk about last night."

"I'd rather not. How did you know I'd be here?"

"Avoiding this won't make it go away. And Miles pointed me this direction."

Avoiding things had been a gift.

"I had a dream about you." His jaw tightened. "The thing is it was more real than any dream I've ever had, it resembled a memory."

She glanced up at him and moved her sunglasses to her head. He definitely seemed shaken up. When he lifted his sunglasses off and clipped them to his shirt, his bloodshot eyes told her what she had already suspected.

"Didn't sleep?"

"Kind of hard to sleep with you in my thoughts."

She knew the feeling. "Maybe you should reconsider the Hogwarts-professor thing. Sure would come in handy now."

He had been far too serious, and she was glad to see the weak smile tug at his lips.

"Yeah, it would. You're a bit pink." He carefully tapped her nose with his finger.

"Forgot the sunblock. Tell me about the dream." She sat in the warm sand and watched the sun's last rays spread out across the calm water.

He dropped down beside her and stretched his

legs out in front of him. "You were dancing around a miniature room. You fell against me after doing some spinning thing. I can only describe it as more than tangible. When I woke, I could feel your hold on my arms where you'd touched me. I couldn't go back to sleep."

She lay on the sand and closed her eyes, rubbing the knot forming in her chest. "What was I wearing?" *If he says a wet, silver dress, I may lose it.*

"A wet, silver dress."

Don't freak. She opened her eyes to him gazing down at her. His dark-blond hair sun-kissed and impeccably messy.

"You dreamt something, too?"

Remain calm. "I fell asleep before I came out here. My dream appears to be very similar to what you described." *More like exactly like what you described.*

"What was I wearing?"

Not much and she had no complaints. "A towel."

He sat up and gazed at her. "Not a dream, then, but a memory."

"Are you psychic?" She sat up.

"Afraid not. Otherwise, I'd be at Hogwarts."

She would have laughed had she not been in panic mode. "Explain it then because I'm about to go off the deep end." She jumped up and paced back and forth in front of him. "Does this sort of thing happen and no one talk about it? Some kind of unnatural déjà vu? This beach could be full of voodoo witches who did some sort of black magic when your rude brother knocked me over." She could hear the slightly hysterical tone in her voice but couldn't seem to stop babbling.

He stopped her by placing his hands on her shoulders. "Last I checked, Lusty Glaze isn't known for black magic. Breathe, slow and deep. Not too fast, you don't want to pass out."

After several deep breaths, she stared into his eyes as the last ray of light sparked around them.

"Better?" He grinned.

"Yeah."

He brushed her hair away from her eyes, and she kissed him. When he embraced her, she melted into his arms. What had come over her? Super-bold move on her part but instinctive. An image of them kissing as a wave washed over them filled her mind's eye.

They dropped to their knees then she pulled out of the sweet ravaging, resonating more than familiar. The crisp scent of him, ocean clean, filled her senses.

"Explain...if you saw it, too," she whispered.

He shook his head. "Kissing you in the sea? I can't." He held her tighter and dropped his head to her shoulder. "I feel more for you in two days than I ever felt for Amber the two years we were together." He pulled them to their feet, keeping her close. "I'll do some research, come up with a theory to start with. It's all I can think to do."

She bit her lip. "Research? Where would you even start?"

He searched the shore and sky with a baffled expression. "Reincarnation?"

"I'll have more time than you will the next few days. I guess reincarnation's a probable theory. But do you really believe it?"

"I never did, but I'm suddenly more open-minded."

Neither one of them moved, pressing against each other like a couple who'd been together for years. She listened to his heartbeat and closed her eyes.

"I don't know why I kissed you."

"I'm not complaining."

She gave him a playful scowl. "I've never jumped into a man's arms and kissed him."

"I'm glad to be the first. But, Kate, we know one

another. I'm not sure how yet."

"The how part is what's unsettling."

A sudden wave of disorientation rippled through her at being on familiar terms with Richard and not recalling the circumstances.

"I have to go." She pulled away from him and bolted off, no second glance behind her. Wouldn't she only run to him? A strange relief washed over her when she realized he hadn't followed her, a little bittersweet because she wanted him to, but she craved a break from the all-consuming mystery.

When she got to Judy's, they were gone, and she went up to her room to take a long hot shower. It didn't wash away the imprints on her soul his touch had left. How could she still feel his hands lingering on her legs and hips? His lips still tasting hers, the summer scent of him all around her?

She got the water as hot as she could stand it and hurried out. She wrapped a towel around her body and pulled out her laptop. She'd plan a day of playing tourist, see some places to help her feel normal, clearheaded, and in touch with reality. She dropped her head to the desk in defeat. Nothing could take him out of her mind.

***

"I must have put too much memory into their déjà vu," Charlotte said.

Henry gave her a crooked grin. "You can't fix this and it only puts you on probation longer." He ran his hand through his dark-brown hair. "You're nothing but trouble, lass." His Scottish burr still made her weak in the knees. "And out of Divine Intervention for good."

She smiled up at him then kissed his cheek. "And you wouldn't have me any other way. I'll figure out how to fix it."

"How are you going to manage? They were only supposed to be given a second chance, not have memories of the afterlife. Now, according to this report"—Henry dropped it on the table in the kitchen—"they're dazed and confused with memories of each other they don't recall."

Charlotte picked up the papers and glanced through them. "My brother belongs with her. I'll figure something out."

Henry lifted her off her feet in a tight hug. "Oh, no you don't. You stay out of it, Charlotte McKendrick. Or you'll have me to deal with."

"Doesn't sound so bad, Mr. McKendrick." She laughed when he threw her over his shoulder and tossed her on the couch.

"I mean it, you stay out of it. You've already done enough." He tickled her until she screamed for mercy and kissed her as he had the day he married her.

Chapter Fourteen
Epiphany

As if dreaming about Richard wasn't intimidating enough, now his bad-mannered brother Will had been added to the fantasy mix. She hesitated outside the hospital entrance. She'd come to talk to him about her dream and ask him if he could give her some information regarding an Ashlee, the name Will called her in the dream last night, before he enveloped her in a passionate embrace.

She had decided to avoid Richard and ignore the whole déjà vu business, but after waking from this latest dream, disregarding him and their obvious attraction to one another became impossible. She'd called the hospital and arranged to meet him when he was off at five. She glanced at her watch—twenty past the hour. She'd paced outside the hospital long enough and regretted having Judy drop her off. Maybe she should have borrowed her car.

Reluctantly, she went in and surveyed the lobby for the hottest doctor in the joint. The sterile environment agitated her, flooding her with sad memories of her dad's many trips to the hospital. She hurried to the exit.

"Kate." He approached her in dark-blue scrubs. "Sorry to make you wait, busy day. You ready, then?" He motioned to the door.

"Sure. Who wouldn't be ready to talk about bizarre dreams, visions, and out-of-this-world chemistry?"

"Not really my cup of tea, either, except for the chemistry you mentioned." He moved his arm around her waist and pulled her close. "Perhaps we shouldn't talk," he whispered over her lips. "Kissing you seems to be the key to more information anyhow."

"You are direct."

"Life's too short not to be." He lifted his chin.

"True, but we shouldn't risk having the big epiphany our affection slams us with in the middle of the ER."

"I disagree. If we have heart attacks, we're in the perfect place to be revived."

She fiddled with her earring, and he released his hold on her.

"All right, then, what did your latest dream reveal?"

They walked outside.

"I'll tell you on the drive to wherever it is we're going."

"May be difficult, since I brought the motorbike today." He pointed to a shiny silver motorcycle. "I had a dream of my own I need to share, not pleasant."

"Oh?"

He frowned. "I have to sign some papers for my father. It shouldn't take long then we can go to my place and talk." He led her to a motorcycle.

"Do you know anyone named Ashlee?"

"No, why?"

"Will called me Ashlee in the dream I had last night."

"Will?"

"Yeah, you were there, too, but he called me Ashlee. The way he studied me, so intense, and just held me. I told him I wasn't Ashlee after he called me Mrs. Bennett, and he kind of disappeared."

He stopped in front of the motorcycle. "Disappeared? Why would he call you Mrs. Bennett?"

"If I knew, I wouldn't be here."

He scratched his head. "He didn't kiss you, did he?"

"No."

"Did you want him to?"

"He's not my type."

"Out of curiosity"—he straddled the bike—"what is your type?"

"Apparently, you are."

"Glad I'm not the only one that's direct." He handed her the helmet. "I borrowed Dr. Richmond's for you."

She put it on then climbed on to the bike.

"Hold on," he shouted over the engine.

She wrapped her arms around him and bowed against his back. It was easy to feel safe and relaxed around him. Her eyes closed when she somehow remembered holding on to him before. Why did she feel like she belonged with him?

Once they were stopped in front of his parents' house, she handed him the helmet then pulled a rubber band from her small pursed draped over her shoulder.

"This is a mansion." She gathered her hair into a ponytail and stood in awe. Palace was an understatement. The place had to be at least 15,000 square feet and could have been showcased in *Town and Country*, with buff-colored stone colonnades running the length of the front façade and an elaborate ornamental garden covering a good hectare of ground.

"It's a bit showy." He set their helmets on the seat and dragged his hand through his hair. "Will's here." He pointed to the silver sports car in the drive. "You should ask him about Ashlee since he won't open up to me. He's been hiding something. Maybe it has something to do with our mystery woman."

"There you are." A striking middle-aged woman walked toward them. "Who's your friend?" She kissed his cheek.

"Mum, this is Kate. Kate, my mum, Veronica."

"Hello."

She recognized the name and the face. Veronica had been a supermodel, one of the hottest catwalkers of her day, splashed across the covers of every big fashion magazine. Even now, she still had a contract with Estee Lauder, aging with uncommon grace.

"Nice to meet you, Mrs. Bennett." She shook her hand, feeling shorter than usual next to his statuesque mother.

"You're American, how lovely. I have some wonderful friends in California." Veronica put an arm around her and led her up the steps to the double doors.

Once inside, Veronica led them to a grand sitting room. "I'll check on dinner then you and I can chat." She smiled then frowned at Richard. "Your father should be in soon. Will and he are agreeing to disagree."

"No worries, Mum. They'll sort it out one of these days."

Veronica gave him a hopeful nod before she left the room.

"Of course, your mom's a supermodel. Explains you and your brother's good looks." She clasped her hands behind her back.

"You think I'm good-looking?"

She blushed. "And your brothers. Tell me about your dream." She sat on one of the three couches in the middle of the room.

He sat beside her. "We were at a restaurant. The place was familiar, but I still can't peg where. I was arguing with Will then you left the room. I watched some deranged man attack you. I shot at him, and he cleared off, but"—he turned to her—"it felt far too real. So, you and I are not going to any restaurants."

"It was only a dream."

He shook his head. "The dreams you and I have are too genuine to only be dreams. I was planning to come by and see you tonight, suggest you go on holiday elsewhere for a while. I could arrange it."

138

"A little extreme, don't you think?"

"No." He took her arms gently. "I have this unexplainable urge to keep you safe from the man in the dream. I could tell he enjoyed harming you, like it triggered some sick pleasure. He had a deep scar across his left cheek. Start thinking of where you'd like to go."

"Now I'm spooked."

"I didn't tell you to frighten you." He stood. "I know it sounds mad, but—"

She stood in front of him. "Okay, I'll go somewhere else for a few days, but you should come with me. We'll get psychiatric help together." She gave him a shaky smile.

He nodded. "Not a bad idea, but I have to work and there's still my brother to figure out. And we aren't crazy, even if we don't have an explanation for this. We aren't hallucinating. I've never felt more real in my life. I know you feel it, too. From both of our dreams, I'm guessing Scarface is possibly connected to Will and whatever he's been hiding. I'll join you as soon as I can."

The front door slammed.

"He's so bloody frustrating!" A distinguished older version of Richard stomped toward them.

"Dad." He gave her a sheepish grin.

"Sorry. I didn't realize you were here with company. I'm Simon." He shook her hand.

"Kate."

"I see your talk with Will went nowhere as usual." He drew in a long breath.

"I'm not even sure why he came by. Best to leave it alone for now. How are you? Long day at the hospital?" Simon went to the bar and poured a drink.

"Always."

"Then let's relax before dinner. I can get to know Kate here. You can sign the papers after."

139

She bit her lip at the thought of dinner with his parents, not while trying to figure out this veiled experience she shared with her favorite doctor. Her *it's okay* gaze at Richard didn't fool him; he seemed to know exactly what her thoughts were.

"We have dinner plans but thank you. I'll sign the papers now, all right?"

"Of course, come to my office, then. We shall chat another time." Simon adjusted his tie before he walked out.

"It shouldn't take long." He followed after his dad but paused. "Feel free to browse around or join my mum in the kitchen."

She gawked around the large room, admiring the bronze sculptures displayed everywhere. The fine paintings on the walls were not like any she'd ever seen at the mall or department stores.

A portrait of a beautiful blonde-haired young woman caught her attention. *Charlotte.* Who's Charlotte? Why had the name come to mind? She had no idea. Whatever her name was, wow she was gorgeous, and angelic and striking, almost a surreal kind of beauty. Her skin was flawless like the rest of her family, and her eyes had a spark of spunk in them she remembered in Will's eyes. Only his spark resembled abrasiveness, where hers was playful.

She moseyed down the hall and into the foyer, thinking Richard must have a sister, but they hadn't really known each other long enough for her to know for sure. When Will walked in and snatched some keys off the marble table near the main entrance, her heart rate sped up. She'd try giving him a chance to prove himself as kind and agreeable and maybe see if he would talk to her. But his expression of disgust had her thinking she should avoid him.

"Remember me?" She walked over to him, letting her curiosity get the better of her.

There was the wounded expression she had seen on his face the day at the beach. His eyes hardened before he quickly glanced away.

"I'm Kate. You ran into me the other day."

"You came out of nowhere." Will darted for the door.

"*I* came out of nowhere?"

He stiffened.

"Have I done something to offend you?"

He pivoted to face her. "I'm having a bad day."

"Is it because I make you uncomfortable or looking at me does?" Nice blurt.

Will leaned closer. "Do you want me to look at you?"

His eyes full of sorrow and the ache in his voice struck her heart cord.

"I'd like to talk." She swallowed intimidation as she stared up at him. He stood a few inches shorter than Richard but still towered over her, projecting a vaguely menacing attitude.

"About?"

"Do you have a girlfriend?"

Will looked away. "Why the sudden interest in my dating status?"

She rolled her eyes. "Okay, this is going to sound crazy and you'll probably laugh, but I had a dream about you." She held her breath.

"I'm thrilled." He plucked at the cuff of his shirt.

"In the dream you called me Ashlee. Mean anything to you?" She sounded crazy.

Will's jaw muscle flexed. "Why would it?"

"I don't know, the way you stared at me. I thought if you did know an Ashlee, she must be important to you. You called me Mrs. Bennett and I don't resemble your supermodel mom."

"I don't interpret dreams." He glanced at his watch. "And I really don't have time for games, love, get to the point."

"I think you're lying. You know an Ashlee, and I remind you of her." Where had the knowledge come from? "And I think you hate me because of it."

He stepped closer to her, and she edged away until her back hit the front door. He placed his hands on the door and bent his head down to hers. "All of this from a dream? Who sent you?" His was voice stiff and low.

"What? No one, I—"

"Last name?" His eyes pierced into hers.

"Adams." The confrontation caused a slightly nauseating sensation from an adrenalin surge, but she plunged ahead anyway. "Richard says you're hiding something. Is it because of her?"

"None of your concern, Kate Adams." Will gripped her arms firmly. "I suggest you tell me the truth, not some nonsense about a dream."

"I told you it would sound crazy."

Will studied her face intensely. "No scars. You don't appear to have had any surgery."

She slapped his hand away when he reached for her chin. "Surgery? Why would I?"

"Ashlee's eyes were brown and her hair more auburn." Will sighed, talking to himself. "But at first glance, you are the ghost of her."

"Really, wait, ghost?"

"Let's discuss this outside, shall we?" Will yanked her by the arm and out the front door. "You're coming with me."

"Like hell I am!" She jerked away from him.

He dragged her to his car. "And you can tell Branson I'm not falling for his trick."

"Who's Branson?"

"You're quite the actress. I could almost believe you really don't know." He opened the car door. "Almost." He shoved her inside.

She kicked her way out and nearly made it to the

front door, but he snatched her from behind.

He covered her mouth and stifled her yelling at him. "I don't want to do this, but you leave me no choice." Will shoved her in the car and, holding her down with one arm and his body weight, reached behind the seat and felt around for something. He covered her mouth and nose with a sweet-smelling rag. Her limbs deadened before her vision and hearing washed out.

Chapter Fifteen
Cheers

"Russell." Will held his phone to his ear as he tore out of his parents' drive at top speed. "I need a check on a Kate Adams."

"Computer's down. I'll get on it as soon as I can. Branson's going to be at Pendennis Castle tonight."

"Good, I'll deliver his Ashlee clone before I kill him."

"Ashlee clone?"

"Mate, she's the ghost of my wife. I had to chloroform her. Branson must have thought he could find me by sending her out as bait. I knocked her down by accident at Lusty Glaze the other day; it's disconcerting how much she resembles Ashlee."

"Crikey. I told you not to take the chloroform."

"I did in case I needed it to torture Branson. Richard fancies the woman, which means my entire family is now in danger. She must have told Branson who I really am. Hurry on the background check. I'm taking her to your place because Richard's been following me and I don't want him anywhere near this mess."

"Damn, Will, things get worse when you react so irrationally. We'll discuss it when you get here."

"Cheers." Will dropped his phone on the dash.

***

Her eyes shot open. Had someone made a toast? Did someone say "cheers"? Why the fancy sports car for travel? Where was she going and who with?

She needed a minute or two to regroup then turned to see Will beside her. Remembering he'd drugged her, she wanted to slap him but thought it best to stay calm until she figured out what to do next because he proved certifiably insane.

Will pulled off to the side of the road and gripped her by the wrists. "Tell me the truth."

"I did." She shook but managed to keep her voice steady.

"Fine. If you won't come clean, sit back and shut up." Will released his grip on her and snatched his phone when it rang. "It's Richard, no doubt wondering where we went off together. I'll have to call him later." He tossed the phone out of her reach. "Have you told Branson who I am?"

"What are you talking about? I don't know a Branson." She remembered Richard's dream and the guy who attacked her in it. "Does he have a scar along his cheek?"

"You know he does. Stop the clueless act. Why don't you do us both a favor and tell me the truth?"

"What are you planning to do with me?"

He scowled. "Torture you until you tell me how you know about my dead wife. No one else does, so you're with Branson until you prove otherwise."

"Your dead wife?" He had a wife? "That's why you called me Mrs. Bennett in my dream. What kind of torture are we talking about?" Was she really having this conversation?

"The painful kind. How much is he paying you?"

Her lips trembled.

"Or are you doing it because you're in love with the sociopath?" Will steered the car on to the road.

"Actually, I think I'm in love with your brother."

"Rubbish, you met him days ago, after conveniently bumping in to me. You keep him and the rest of my family out of your game. Does Branson know who I really am?"

"Who you really are? What the hell are you talking about? Are you a rebel agent or something?"

"What I am is none of your concern."

They drove in deafening silence until they reached their destination—a modern-style home, far off the beaten path.

He opened her car door and smirked. "After you."

She slowly stepped out and gazed around ready to make a run for it. Long after dark now, it wasn't like she'd know where they were anyway or where to run to.

Will pushed her toward the front door and she went inside.

He jerked her by the arm and led her down the stairs. At the bottom, Will unlocked a door and shoved her inside a dark room and slammed the door.

Her hands slid over the walls in hopes of finding a light switch. After a few minutes, she gave up and slid down the wall to the cold, concrete floor and sniffled. It wasn't the dark she feared; being out of control broke her every time. And how could Richard be related to such a slimeball like Will?

She composed herself. Her stomach growled, now past dinnertime, and she had only toast for breakfast today. Hunger came over her.

Richard must be completely baffled as to why she would leave with Will. And what would Will tell him? Her eyes couldn't adapt in the pitch-black room. She closed her eyes and waited for Will to come for her.

***

"What if you're wrong about her?" Russell sat across from Will on a chair.

"I'm not."

"Why the rubbish about a dream?"

Will shook his head. "I don't know what's in Branson's sick head or where he would find Ashlee's clone, but I'm not taking any chances. I want to end this and get back to my daughter."

"I'm not too keen on your method of kidnapping your brother's girlfriend. Have you checked in on Madelyn lately?" Russell asked.

"A few days ago. She's trying to walk already." Will grinned.

"Eleven months old...sounds right. She'll keep you busy once it happens."

"I end this tonight so Maddie can keep me busy; I miss her. And I may have overreacted in regards to her, but, Russell, when you see her, you'll understand. I can't be wrong about this. It *is* Branson playing his sick game."

"Perhaps." Russell stood and gazed down the stairs. "Why were you at your parents? I thought you told me you were never going there."

Will rubbed his eyes. "I wanted to see them in case."

"In case?"

"In case something happens to me."

Russell frowned. "I was right, then. You do have a death wish."

Will shrugged. "I'm too tired to know what I have."

"Once we end Branson, you and I are going straight over to your parents and explaining everything to them. Simon is the closest thing to a brother I have, and I'm sick of lying. He may never speak to me again." He sighed. "We should feed her, offer her a drink at least. Because if you are wrong about her, Richard will come after you if you are anything less than hospitable."

"You can if you like. I'm steering clear of her until I take her to Pendennis. There's only so much of being around her I can take. And he can try. My little brother has no idea who she really is. He only met her on the shore when I did."

"I think I'll go down out of curiosity." Russell sauntered down the stairs.

***

Will retreated to the spare room he always stayed in at Russell's and fell on the bed. Exhausted didn't even come close to the fatigue he dwelled in. And Kate cut him deep. He ached for Ashlee daily, and seeing Kate only intensified his pain. What was he doing? It had all happened so fast, and before he knew it, he had chloroformed her and was on his way here.

And Russell had one thing right. Will did have a death wish. No, he didn't think of ending his own life, but if while attempting to end Branson's he died, he welcomed it. In death, he would be with Ashlee. Whether it be an endless existence of nothing or an eternity of some after life with her didn't matter. Wherever she existed, he wanted to be with her.

When his phone rang and he glanced at it and saw Richard's number, he knew he had to lie to him and most likely hurt him to keep him away from all of this rubbish. He despised pretending to be the arrogant bastard he portrayed, but once again it was necessary.

"I know why you're calling. I can assure you I am providing Kate good care, if you know what I mean."

"You unbelievable bastard! You expect me to believe she left with you?"

"Turns out, I'm more her type than you are. Apparently, she even dreams of me. Now be a good brother and accept defeat and leave me alone so I can get on with what you so rudely interrupted."

"Let me talk to her! And when I get my hands on you..."

"Cheers." Will hung up and turned his ringer off.

It was all for the best, he reminded himself. He couldn't lose anyone else ever again the way he had lost Ashlee. And contrary to what Richard thought, Will loved his brother very much.

***

Kate stood when the key turned in the lock.

"I'm Russell." He flipped a switch on the outside of the door, and the light filled the room.

She squinted at him.

"Will must have forgotten to turn the light on. Are you hungry?"

She would spit venom at him if she could.

"I doubt he forgot." She turned her face away from Russell.

He pulled some handcuffs from his pocket. "I'm not going to hurt you. I have to do this until we get the background check on you, shouldn't be much longer." He secured the cuffs on her wrists, and a sad expression came to his face. "Your resemblance to Ashlee is haunting."

"Will mentioned it." She stomped up the stairs when Russell followed.

"You don't seem the type to be connected to Branson, but from what Ashlee mentioned, he's very charming. Did he charm you into haunting Will?" Russell handed her a glass of water.

She sipped it as well as she could, being in handcuffs. "I don't know anyone named Branson. I already told Will."

"And your interest in Richard?"

"Is none of your business," she huffed.

"Fair enough. How about a sandwich?"

"No." She didn't know what to think of Russell, but she sure as hell wouldn't take any food from him. "I don't take food from bad guys."

Russell raised his brow. "I'm the bad guy? You sure?"

"If you're involved with Will, yes."

"It's all perception, Kate, and yours couldn't be more off."

"Really? I'm pretty sure drugging someone and kidnapping them makes one a bad guy. Not to mention the prison cell I came out of." How she got that out without stuttering was a miracle.

Russell opened the bag of bread sitting on the counter. "I'll make you a sandwich anyway; it's past dinnertime. And you're either a very good actress or completely innocent. I'm hoping for the latter."

He put together a ham and cheese sandwich until Will walked into the kitchen. She scowled at him, but he ignored her for the moment.

"What's with the computer?" Will said.

"I'll see if it's up. You can sit with her while she eats." Russell uncuffed her then walked out.

"Don't come near me." She turned her back to Will when he motioned toward her with the sandwich Russell had made.

"Have it your way." He sat at the table. "But you should eat. You'll want to have your strength. You'll need it to explain your failure to Branson. I'll let you, before I kill him."

Hungry, she stared at the sandwich now set in front of Will.

"You're going to feel horrible when you realize I'm not working for Branson."

Will sighed. "Perhaps, but a little guilt never hurt anyone."

"So you're going to turn me over to some crazy man?"

"Yes."

She glanced at the sandwich when her stomach rumbled. "I need to call Richard."

"Ah yes, we spoke. Told him you had pleasant dreams of me and I was the perfect host. He took it quite well."

Enough. How dare he hurt Richard! She snatched a plate off the counter then flung it at his head. Time to fight and get out of here. Standing around waiting to be tortured was no longer an option.

Will ducked and laughed. "No worries. It isn't the first time a lady's left him for me."

She grabbed a sugar dish from the table and threw it at him. She howled with joy when the dish smacked him on the cheek. She darted toward the front door.

Will brought the heel of his hand to his cheek. "You're bloody mad!" He lunged at her.

"Easy." Russell jumped in front of Will. "I'll take you to your room." He gripped her by the arm and pulled her downstairs.

She wiped the tear running down her cheek.

He handed her a small bag. "There's a change of clothes in the bag. Get ready; you'll leave for Branson within the hour."

***

Richard stood in the shower dazed. It didn't make sense. Kate wouldn't leave with Will.

He'd gone to Will's place to find him gone as usual. And the rubbish Will told him about her falling for him when he phoned, he hated him.

Stepping out of the shower, he wrapped a towel around his waist and thought to his dream the night before. It spooked him and not much did.

The man in his dream had beaten and nearly killed her. Then he shot at him and the demon disappeared. Wherever they were in the dream, he'd been there but he couldn't quite place it.

"Think," he mumbled to himself and pulled on his jeans.

It weakened him to suspect Kate in danger and not know where she may be. Will must have gotten her involved in whatever secret he'd been hiding, but why?

The constant speculation was driving him mad. He pulled a shirt on and paced around his bedroom. Something seemed off, and he had a sinking feeling it had everything to do with his dream.

***

"There has to be something I can do to help Richard remember Pendennis. We went years ago for the family sleepover. So wonderful. We had supper and listened to spooky stories before bedding down for the night," Charlotte said to Ashlee.

"Sounds nice." Ashlee was browsing through the Guidebook for Communicating with the Living. "Maybe you could do the Dreams Whisper True greeting. I've tried with Will but no luck. I love the man, but he's so thick-headed. He's going to get Kate killed."

Charlotte sighed. "And if she dies before her time, well Will won't like the consequences for his soul when he does die."

Ashlee shook her head. "I saw his name on the new arrival's list. What can we do to stop it?"

Charlotte put her arm around Ashlee. "Nothing if it's his time."

"But my baby, I want him to take care of Maddie."

"Madelyn will be fine. And I would do the Dreams Whisper True greeting you mentioned earlier to Richard if he were asleep, but there's hardly time and he's not resting while he's got the urge to find Kate. Do you think Will is really going to drag her to Branson? Is he so dense?"

"Not usually, but he's not thinking straight. Watching it all unravel is torture." Ashlee gave a stern eye to the hologram of Will getting ready to take Kate to Branson."

"Come on." Charlotte huffed. "Let's go talk to Perry about seeing Will's guardian angel again."

Chapter Sixteen
From Bad to Worse

"Call me as soon as you get the report on Kate." Will straightened his tie, now dressed in a suit. He often kept clothes at Russell's to fall back on.

"You sure you don't want me to come?" Russell yawned.

"It's my battle. You've helped plenty. And I'll phone if I need you."

"Mate, I've been where you are, and sometimes the revenge and justice part of avenging your dead wife muddles your senses. I don't have a good feeling about taking her to Branson unless we know for certain she is in fact working for him. Let's be done with going after Branson if we get the report and she's clean."

Will put his gun inside the shoulder holster he wore over his shirt then put his suit jacket on. "I'll stay near her to protect her *if* I'm wrong. I'm too close to killing Branson to let her muck it up. And listen to what you're saying? You never gave up on avengement for Elena."

"You leave my wife out of this. My situation and yours are much different. I've told you getting my sense of recompense didn't make anything better but worse after. "Will." Russell put his hand on Will's shoulder. "You know I've always thought of you as my own and why I'm telling you to wait. Let's see what information I get on Kate first. You still have a child to think of and live for. If I hadn't lost my baby girl, too, I don't believe I would have pursued Elena's killer."

"I appreciate the pep talk, but you know I have to do this." Will made his way downstairs and unlocked Kate's door.

The innocence adorning her face hit him with a shot of regret. *Was* he thinking clearly? No time for doubts now. He'd come too far to start rethinking things. Could Russell be right?

At first glance, he wanted to hold her but only because the image of Ashlee appeared to him in the moment. He blinked hard to clear his senses.

She stood from the lone chair in the room and attempted civility, in hopes of persuading Will to change his mind.

"Shall we?" Will raised a brow.

"I'd rather not. Keep me in this room forever if you want, but don't take me to Branson. And sorry about the black eye," she lied, but thought the apology may soften the beast.

Will brought one finger to his eye. "I see the dress fits."

She modified the thin straps of the black cocktail dress. "You always keep spare women's clothes lying around?'

"Only for these types of occasions."

"Please." She inched forward. "Don't make me do this. If Richard's dream is a premonition, Branson will attack me and may end up killing me."

"Enough with the bloody dreams." He gripped her by her arm and marched up the stairs.

For a second, she thought about fighting him off but figured she'd have a better chance when they were away from Russell and in a public setting. She would have to try and fool him, let him believe she'd succumbed to his unwise plan.

"Where are we going?" she asked after they'd been driving a few minutes.

"Pendennis Castle. But you already knew."

"You mentioned Ashlee was your wife and dead when you kidnapped me…I'm sorry for your loss and swear I have nothing to do with this Branson guy."

Will shot her an annoyed scowl.

She rubbed her temples and her stomach growled. A castle would be a unique place to die. She tilted her head up to gaze out the window and stared at the night sky. She didn't know what else she could say to change Will's mind; he seemed far too stubborn anyway.

When Will stopped the car in the parking lot, she crossed her legs. "I'm not getting out."

He seemed to consider letting her stay but then gave her a hard glare before exiting the vehicle and pulling her out of the car.

Which way to run? The castle was surrounded by a large grassy area and sat on a cliff. Green, purple, and pink lights helped display it in the dark, and she silently thanked the shadows for serving her with some suitable hiding places when she did have a chance to run. Should she wait until they got inside or take off now?

Will put his hands firmly on her waist and pulled her close. "We do this my way. You stay by me until I tell you otherwise."

Running would come when they got closer to the castle, then.

"What's your plan?" She sighed.

"Kill Branson."

"And if he kills me?"

"He won't, not straightaway. You're his second chance at Ashlee."

The urge to slap him burned through her hand. "Ouch." She bent over and grabbed her ankle, pretending to have twisted it.

Will moved his hand to her arm.

She kicked off her heels then positioned them in each hand with the heels pointing up.

"What's Richard doing here?" She bluffed, pointing in the distance and pulled her arm from his hold so she could attack him with her high heels.

The first swipe she gave him cut across his cheek.

157

She slammed the other heel into his side before kicking him in the groin. Seizing the advantage of surprise, she shot off like a cannon, but within a few seconds, his cursing shouts echoed behind her.

If she hadn't been running for her life, it would have been a moment both triumphant and hilarious. Dodging Will tested harder than she anticipated, and sprinting across the castle grounds barefoot didn't help. Once she had him on the wrong track by running down the moat and climbing up and over the bridge in the other direction, she darted off toward the cliff.

Taking a short break to catch her breath, a small cottage caught her eye off in the distance. No time to hesitate so she ran toward it. She suddenly had an image of some scar-faced lunatic coming after her, thanks to Richard's dream. Staying away from the castle seemed the best option, especially if there was a restaurant there. If his dream held true, the cottage had to be the better alternative.

A few lights appeared through the windows of the small house. If she could get inside, she could call Richard. Then again, they hadn't really exchanged numbers yet. She'd have to call the hospital and ask them for it. Her feet were sore, worn, and dirty by the time she stood at the red door of the stone building, but she put her heels on anyway.

Knocking would be the polite thing to do, but with Will after her, she barged in instead. Moving to grip the doorknob, she hesitated. But then the thought of Scarface had her inside in a jiff. The group of four men gathered in the dimly lit living room ogled at her.

"Sorry to barge in. Could I use the phone?" She bit her lip.

All eyes wandered to a ruggedly handsome cigar-smoking cowboy who needed a shave. He gave her a tip of the Stetson hat he wore. "Come in, darlin'. We're wrapping things up."

She did a quick face scan for any scars while the others gathered their things— duffel bags and cash from what she observed then hustled out.

"I didn't mean to break up your party." She searched the room for a phone. Were they playing poker?

"Are you in some kind of trouble?" He motioned her to the couch and rubbed his hand over his stubble.

She glanced out the window, knowing she had to make up something. "Blind date from hell. I'll stand, thanks." She stayed close to the door.

"Never been a fan of blind dates myself." He went to the kitchen and returned with bottled water for her. "You're not from around here." He lifted the hat from his head and set it on the couch.

"Thanks." Once she got a big gulp of water down, she shook her head. "On vacation."

When she got closer, he had a deep scar along his left cheekbone. Positive self-talk rationalized nothing but a freaky coincidence to Richard's dream and shook it off. Richard didn't mention the creep growing a goatee, so this guy should be safe. And right now, anyone other than Will would do. But she'd stay close to the door anyhow.

"I travel plenty in my line of work but don't do much sightseeing." He was polite, but something about him made her uncomfortable; the scar did stand out. Not wanting to be judgmental about a guy a little rough around the edges, she tried to relax. And wouldn't Branson be English? This guy resembled a good old boy from the U.S.A.

She rested a hand on her hip and gazed down at her dirt-covered feet. "I'd better make the call." She glanced around for the phone.

"In the kitchen."

"Thanks." She darted to the kitchen and called information to the hospital Richard worked at. They wouldn't give her his number but assured her they'd get the message to him. She debated on whether to hang out with the cowboy or take her chances with Will outside.

She went over to the window and didn't see Will lurking around.

"Would you like to sit?" The cowboy moved beside her.

"No thanks," she folded her arms.

"You can hold up here as long as you need to." He gave her a small grin.

Something about the way his eyes avoided contact with hers caught her attention. His expression, sad and irritated.

"I really am sorry about the intrusion."

He rubbed his thumb across his upper lip. "I'm not."

"Would you mind if I use the bathroom?" She needed a minute to come up with a plan, clear her head without the cowboy around.

"Down the hall." He pointed.

She walked in the bathroom and glanced at herself in the mirror. Frazzled and windblown hair aside, she pulled off the Bond girl role with success, only lacking a gun and some kick-boxing skills. After she washed her face and decided against rinsing her feet off in the tub, she let out a deep sigh. Maybe she'd call the hospital again, see if they got the message to Richard.

When she came out, she found the southern gentleman in the kitchen. "I have some tea for you, thought you could use it while you wait for your friend."

"Thanks...I'm sorry, I didn't get your name?" She reached for the mug he offered, thinking how thoughtful he was.

"Cale." He offered his hand. "And you are?"

"Kate."

"It's nice to meet you, Kate."

"Same."

"So, what line of work are you in?"

She took in a deep breath.

"Sorry, I'm being nosy about a fellow American."

She should get used to her reality. "I was a ballet dancer, in New York."

"Was?" He pulled out a chair for her at the table.

"Thanks. Yes, I'm not sure what I'm going to do now. I'll figure it out."

He sat across from her. "I don't mean to pry, but you seem upset about not dancing anymore. What changed it?"

"You don't want to hear my pity party." She sipped the warm tea.

"Sure do." When he grinned, his hazel eyes beamed genuine.

"A serious car accident on New Year's Eve, injuries were life altering. My ballet career's over." She finally said it out loud. Why did she tell him? He seemed interested and easy to talk to. Maybe the lack of emotional attachment made admitting things to a stranger easier than sharing your pain with someone close.

"Sorry to hear. Were you hit by a drunk driver?"

"No, I take the title of careless driver after I left my cousin's wedding in Vegas."

"I'll be damned. I was in Las Vegas New Year's Eve. What hotel?" He lit the cigar he pulled out of his shirt pocket and leaned back in his chair.

"Off the strip, up Mount Charleston."

"I stayed at The Mount Charleston Hotel, some coincidence." He gave her a curious grin.

She turned her face away, not wanting to stare at his scar.

"It's not pretty is it?" He rubbed his finger along the scar from cheekbone to mouth.

"Had to have hurt." She cringed.

He nodded. "Something fierce. But I don't regret helping the woman."

"You helped someone and they cut you?"

"Stopped a mugger. The lowlife stabbed me here." He cuffed his sleeve up and showed her his jagged scar along his forearm. "Then sliced me across the face."

"Lucky for her, you showed up."

He shrugged.

She thought of Will and glanced at the front door.

"I won't let the date of yours in here."

"Thank you. Hopefully, Richard will be here soon."

"Who's he?"

"The man I should be on a date with."

"And the one you're running from?"

"Will."

He took a long drag of the cigar and blew out smoke. "Why were you with Will, then, if you want to be with Richard?"

"Will kind of forced the date on me."

"I see." His eyes studied her thoughtfully. "You've got a few scars of your own." He pointed to her knee. "From the accident?"

She nodded.

"Wait a minute. There was an accident a few miles from the hotel, with some idiots racing motorcycles. You were the one they ran into?"

"Yes, and we kind of ran into each other."

"I remember driving past it after the ambulance transported you all to the hospital. You were lucky to be alive from what I remember of the wrecked car on fire and all."

She *was* lucky to be alive.

"So, what do you do?" She became distracted by the clock ticking on the wall. She'd been here for half an hour.

After snuffing out his cigar in the ashtray, he tapped his fingers on the table. "I'm an independent contractor. I train others to do what I do."

"Which is?"

"Classified information." He winked.

"You work for the government?"

"I work for whoever hires me."

"Must be exciting. You mentioned traveling a lot, like it?"

"Most of the time but miss being home in Alabama."

Her head felt fuzzy. She leaned forward and rubbed her temples.

"You all right, darlin?"

"I'm hungry. I haven't eaten much today." Panic came over her. She stood and walked to the living room. "I'm going to head to the restaurant and wait for Richard there. Thanks again. I really appreciate your hospitality." Richard had told her they were in a restaurant in his dream, so there had to be one here.

"Afraid I can't let you." Cale blocked her path to the door. "Will's still out there."

She couldn't think straight, had he put something in her tea? "I'll be okay. What's your last name? So that I can tell Richard who to thank for being such a kind host." The urge to leave increased exponentially.

"Branson."

Her blood ran cold, and she struggled to keep her voice relaxed. "I've taken up too much of your time already." She was light-headed.

His eyes changed from caring and concerned to dark and cold. His brow creased when he stepped toward her. "The funny thing is you weren't scared of me until I told you my last name."

She shook her head still feeling off-balance. "I'm not scared of you." Horrified would be a better word.

"I can tell you are, Kate. I can sense your fear. It's

one of my hobbies." He turned off the lamp.

She calculated the distance to the door, but he hovered. She searched the room for another way out.

Branson approached her with a wicked smile. "The other thing about you, darlin', is your resemblance to my ex. The only reason I let you come in and break up my business meeting. Now, how are you going to make it up to me?"

She reared away from him, stopping when her back hit the wall. "Richard will be here soon."

"What I have in mind isn't going to take long. We'll be done before he shows up. You should be relaxed by now from the tea."

He had drugged her. Good thing she'd only had a few sips. "So, I resemble your ex-girlfriend?" she blurted, trying to buy time.

"Ashlee betrayed me." He tenderly traced the lines of her face. His expression, full of regret for a moment then his eyes turned black. "But she shouldn't have left. I've never liked it much when people I care about run out on me."

She swallowed the bile in her throat. Had he been abandoned as a child? He had to have been raised by a sadistic cult in the deep woods of Alabama. "She left you?" If she could keep him talking, buy some time, maybe Will would find her.

He nodded, still caressing her face. "She was euphoric about it, as if she delighted in what she had done. Then she ran off with some Brit named Colin. She loved him but was only ever supposed to love me." He ran his finger along her jaw bone. "You could be her twin."

"Are you going to kill me?" Her voice shook.

"Are you going to try and run off?"

"No."

"Good, why don't we sit, then?" He dragged her to the couch and pulled her onto his lap. "I've told you too much to try and charm you," he whispered in her ear. "Why don't we make a deal."

The man is a psychopath. Had he escaped some psycho ward before Ashlee met him? She contemplated what her next move would be, but her thoughts were lethargic and foggy. The drug he had spiked her tea with had dulled her ability to think clearly. Even worse, she felt as if she was a puppet, only able to move on command.

"I'll let you live." He lifted her hair from her neck and kissed her shoulder.

She cowered and fought the urge to puke.

"But only if you forget about Richard and stay with me."

Say what he wants to hear. "Okay, but the scar, you didn't help any woman, did you?" Her voice still shook.

He gave her a dark smirk. "No. I enjoyed watching the lie bring light to your pretty face." Branson moved his mouth over her ear. "Ashlee did it, before I killed her."

Run! An ear-piercing alarm went off inside her. From somewhere deep inside, she summoned all her strength and pulled out of his lap. She made it only as far as the door handle before he fisted her hair and jerked her head back.

"I thought you said you wouldn't run off?" He gripped her by the throat and squeezed until she gasped for air. "You brought this on yourself."

He gripped her by the throat and lifted her off her feet. She kicked and flailed until he threw her to the floor.

Coughing and gasping for air, she spoke up. "Colin sent me, Ashlee's alive."

"Colin? He thought I'd think you were Ashlee, didn't he? At first glance, it is uncanny. But I squeezed the last breath out of her myself. She's six feet under."

She inched for the door again.

He shoved her against the wall and dug his fist into her gut. "Now tell me more about Colin's, Richard's or Will's plan? Dr. Richard Bennett, right? I heard your plea over the phone for him to pick you up."

The reality of her situation, truly grim, had her recalling some talk show she'd watched months earlier on what to do in a situation where you're assaulted or kidnapped. It was better to fight and try and get away because they'd most likely murder you.

"Will's going to kill you," she half spoke, half wheezed out.

Branson smiled. "Kill me? Laughable. Has he been the one following me for months now?"

In her mind, she pleaded for Richard to hurry but realized the futility of the situation. If he did get the message from the hospital, she doubted he'd make it in time to save her.

Ironically, her best chance was Will, but he probably went hunting for her inside the castle.

She feared the same fate as Ashlee. Unless something changed soon. The thought spurred her to action. Although her senses were confused, she raged inside and adrenalin pushed her to fight. What to do? She'd grab something and throw it at him, but he still had her arms. When she squirmed away from him, he only tightened his hold on her. The loud banging on the door startled him.

"Kate! Are you in there?" Richard shouted.

"Richard!" she yelled. When Branson loosened his hold on her and lunged for the door, she grabbed a bookend from the shelf next to them and threw it at his leg and ran to the opposite end of the house and found refuge in the bedroom. With trembling hands, she locked the door then went to the window and searched for a way to open it. With no time for her to turn on a light, she hunted for anything to throw through it.

Branson pounded on the door when she picked up the lamp and launched it through the glass. Then she kicked off her heels and used them to knock the loose glass from the window. Her head still felt groggy but she pushed through it.

Behind her, she became dimly aware of the door being kicked open. Branson pulled her by the waist when she balanced halfway out the window. Pieces of glass sliced over her arms and hands before he slammed her to the floor. The blood dripped from her mouth and her cheek tasted like metal bone. She cried in agony when he kicked her in the ribs.

He lifted her up and slapped her across the face. Acting solely on instinct, she thrust one of her shoes at his head, aiming the heel at his eye, but he turned around and the blow never fully connected. Instead, her dance training ignited and she let the momentum spin her around. Coming out of the turn, she leapt onto the bed. It must resemble a dark ballet, she thought while she continued to put space between them. Like some twisted scene where a fair creature was mocked and bullied by a menacing monster. If she could only thrust one of her high heels into his temple, she thought again to the talk show with self-defense moves, it would kill him.

He laughed at her, low and haunting. His fists went up to strike at her, and she dropped into a fetal position on the bed.

Gunfire rang in her ears from outside the window. Branson swore, and she closed her eyes, unable to face another attack. She squinted at him when he grabbed his right shoulder now soaked in blood.

He let out a harsh breath. "I'm not done with you." He tore out of the bedroom and disappeared.

She closed her eyes and huddled in the corner.

Richard wrapped his arms around her. "I've got

you, love."

She clung to him, unable to stop the uncontrollable shiver of fear still coursing through her blood. The familiar man she adored had finally come to her aid.

"I'm okay." Her teeth chattered.

"Toughest I've seen. Come on, then." He lifted her into his arms and when gunfire rang outside, she gripped onto the collar of his shirt. Tears ran over her blood-stained cheeks. "I'm not okay."

"I know, but you will be. Will's going after Branson. Let's get you to the hospital."

She shook her head when he carried her out of the room and to the front door.

"No. He'll follow us there," she half whispered, gripping her side.

Will ran through the front door and over to them. When he saw Kate, he clenched his jaw. "I told you to stay with me."

The regret and pain on his face didn't matter to her. She lunged at him and punched him in the face then latched onto Richard again.

"Kate's not the only one going to get satisfaction, but I'll spare you until later." He walked out.

Will came up beside them with his gun still drawn. "Hospital is the first place he'll check. Russell has what you need at his place."

Richard nodded. "I expect a full explanation."

"Fair enough," Will said as they got in separate cars and drove to Russell's.

***

Branson raced off in his car, gripping his shoulder. He snatched his phone from his pocket and cursed under his breath. Colin was Will Bennett—he needed to get information on him right away.

He called his most trusted ally and set the phone down after putting it on speaker. "Ray. I'm headed your way. I need information on Will or William Bennett. And call the doc to meet me at your place. I have a bullet in my shoulder."

"You got it. I'm in front of the computer now. Give me a minute. What happened, sir?"

"I found Ashlee's man. Once you have the info, I'm going to teach him a lesson. And his brother?"

"Jack or Richard? I see they are a wealthy family and high profile. The sons of Simon and Veronica Bennett."

"Find Jack, we'll snatch him and let Arty show him a few of his new toys. Send Hag and Sykes to get him. Take him to the shack."

Branson ended the call and laughed out loud. He pulled down the visor and sneered at Ashlee's picture. He had taken it when they toured London and she was in front of Hampton Court Palace. "I've got your man, Ashlee. And now I'm gonna get Kate to join you in hell."

Chapter Seventeen
Clarify

Richard fastened her seat belt and covered her with his jacket before starting the engine and pulling out of the drive.

She closed her eyes, still shaking and fighting the urge to throw up. The blood in her mouth didn't help. Her ribs ached at being crushed and pliable, and the cut in her dress where his steel-tipped boots had pierced through stained with blood. The cut didn't ooze with blood, but she couldn't bear to study it too close.

He stayed quiet.

"I'm glad you found me." She turned to him, surprised at how raspy her voice sounded. But then again, Branson had strangled her.

He cocked his head. "I was on my way to Pendennis when the hospital phoned me with your message. I was relieved to be on the right track, having finally remembered the inside of the castle from the dream but when the nurse confirmed it with her phone call, I've never been more scared."

She covered her mouth with her hand. "Would you pull over? I think I'm going to be sick."

He did as she asked.

She unsnapped the seat belt and leaned out the door after she opened it.

He held her hair back then handed her a bottle of water from behind his seat.

"Branson put something in my tea, made me tired, dizzy. I feel better now."

"Glad it left your system."

She swished the water around her sore mouth and spit. After a minute and a small drink, she moaned.

"Thanks, not only for the water but for saving me."

"I only wish I'd arrived sooner. How did Will get you to leave with him?"

She fastened the seat belt, and he pulled the car onto the road. "He shoved me in his car then I think he chloroformed me."

"What?"

"You heard me."

"I'm going to kill him." He sped up.

She gave a bitter laugh because she did not want to sob but stopped because her side hurt. "I feel the same, but let's hear what he has to say first."

"How can you defend him? After all he's caused to happen to you? He's dead."

"You can't kill your own brother. Besides, you're a doctor not an assassin. I'm not defending him, but he had a reason for what he did. He thought I worked for Branson."

"True. Maybe I'll kick his arse. Nicely done, by the way, on the jab you gave him." He grinned over at her.

She carefully touched her cheek. "It made me feel better. He let it slip when he kidnapped me, Ashlee was his wife, she's dead."

"His wife? Are you certain? Will's not the marrying kind."

"It came from his mouth. Branson killed Ashlee. Said she gave him no choice. I can see how he fooled Ashlee with his charm. He's got the 'good old country boy act' down. And he's not hard to look at if you're into rugged cowboys."

He turned the car left. "I'm impressed. You're terribly calm for someone who's been assaulted."

She knew why she came across as composed. "You calm me. Being around you soothes me. But don't be too impressed yet. Once I see the damage, I may pass out. I'm relieved to be away from the psychopath."

"No worries." He kissed her hand. "I'm your bodyguard. And believe the time has come for you to go on holiday somewhere else. Have you ever been to Paris?"

"Does the Paris Hotel in Vegas count?"

"Absolutely not. Paris it is."

After fifteen minutes and him telling her all of the places she'd have to visit in France, they pulled in front of Russell's.

He lifted her out of the car and carried her inside.

"Come this way." Russell led them up the front steps and inside the house. "Will rang, explained the situation."

He ushered them through the living room, and she groaned. "You're not going to put me in the dungeon, are you?"

Russell led them up the stairs. "Not this time and Will's responsible, not me."

"Dungeon?" Richard pulled her closer. "I'm going to torture Will."

Russell opened the door to his room then touched the side of the fireplace, when the wall slid open.

"I can't wait to hear why you have secret compartments in your house." He shook his head, following Russell down a wide and winding staircase as the wall closed behind them.

"I have a friend who is Interpol. Think of me like Bruce Wayne without the bat suit. I've used my connections to set things up as I've needed them here."

At the bottom of the stairs, a miniature ER greeted them. He set her on the bed gently. "When there's more time, I definitely want to hear about it." He found the sink and washed his hands.

He looked to Russell. "I'll examine her first and hope you'll have what I need."

"Here's a gown." Russell dropped it next to her.

She frowned. The dress was skin tight and at the moment, with every muscle screaming in pain, she didn't think she could move her little finger, let alone the contortions required to take off the cocktail gown. "Can we cut this off?"

Russell walked across the room then handed some scissors to Richard.

He started at the hem of the dress, mid-thigh, and cut along the side of her body. When he snipped the last stitch of material under her arm, he dropped the scissors on the metal tray Russell had moved beside the bed and helped her put the hospital-style gown on.

Once covered, she carefully peeled the dress off and tossed it on the floor.

"Where do you feel the most pain?" He inspected her hand and studied the cuts on her arm.

"My neck"—she reached for her throat—"and ribs."

"Is an X-ray possible?" He brushed her hair back from her face.

"Yes, in the other room."

"Stethoscope?" He held his hand out.

Russell handed him the one around his neck.

"I'm going to check your lungs then we'll get an X-ray. So far"—he paused and had her breathe in and out a few times while he listened to her lungs—"I think they may be broken or badly bruised. And I need to see what's bleeding through." He pulled the covers up to her waist then lifted her gown up to see her ribs. "Damn." He frowned at Russell. "She'll need stitches."

Russell inspected her wound. "I'll get what you need."

"You allergic to anything?" Richard asked.

A quiver of fear raced up her spine, and her heart started pounding at the harmless question. She recognized the symptoms—the start of a panic attack. How come she could face off a sociopathic killer then fall apart at a routine medical question? Maybe this was still her psyche's way of dealing with her encounter with Branson.

"My heart. I'm okay, I'm okay, I'm okay," she whispered and closed her eyes, reminding herself she only felt exaggerated fear.

"Have you had a panic attack before?"

"Unfortunately." She held her hand to her chest and managed some slow deep breaths.

"I have just the thing." Russell went to a stainless-steel cabinet and came over to her with a small pill.

She waved shaky hands at him. "I don't like to take pills. It's going away."

"I want an IV in her, she's most likely dehydrated," Richard said.

Russell started pulling stuff from drawers. "I'll get her some ice for her ribs and an anti-inflammatory."

"No needles, please." Her voice shook, still waiting for the dread meter inside to stop.

Richard raised a brow. "You won't feel a thing."

"I don't believe you." She welcomed the warm calm from the episode being over.

Once she was X-rayed, stitched, and bandaged by her favorite doctor, he handed her a cup of ice water.

"Is she all right then?" Will came in from the stairs.

Richard lunged at him and threw him against the wall, knocking over the metal tray in the process.

"Bruised ribs, multiple lacerations, and stitches! Not to mention the imprint of Branson's hand on her neck. No, she's not all right!"

She had second thoughts of glancing in the mirror anytime soon after Richard's rundown but did want to hear Will's side of things.

"Let him explain," she choked out.

"Only because she wants you to." He removed his hands from Will's collar.

Will stepped away from him and moved next to Russell.

"I've heard this before." Russell started for the

stairs. "I'll get her something to eat."

"You remember Evan Grant," Will began.

"Your armed forces mate?"

Will nodded. "He had a drug problem while we served together. A few of us tried to help him and he seemed to get it under control. Years after we were out, he rang me and asked me to meet him at some dodgy pub in Brixton but to take the bus and under no circumstances should I drive my own car. His paranoia definitely piqued my curiosity, and I became bored doing business for Father and figured why not."

"He finally showed, still a mess. Then he spewed information I thought rubbish at the time, told me about how he had to bring some American named Ashlee to the creep. Evan owed Branson money, and if he found Ashlee, Branson would forget the debt he owed him. But Evan had a moment of conscience and decided to hide her from Branson instead. Desperate, yes but not a kidnapper. He asked me for the money to pay Branson. I told him I'd get it for him, but he would have to go into a rehab center to get clean. A few blokes walked in. I helped him fight them off after they interrogated him and he told them Ashlee ran off with some man named Colin. By the time I got to Evan in the alley, it was too late."

She flinched and sat up. "Branson thinks your name's Colin. Told me Ashlee ran off with you."

Will nodded.

"Then you went to help Ashlee and got caught in the game?" Richard asked.

"No, I decided to ignore what he told me, thinking him high. I wanted to get the bastards who killed Evan, so I phoned the police anonymously, not wanting to get on Branson's radar."

"Then you went to Ashlee?" she asked.

Will shook his head. "I thought on it a few days then browsed through his phone." Will paused when a

176

melancholy mood came to his face. His forehead wrinkled. "It had a number for Ashlee and I phoned her." His voice was soft now, almost a whisper. "She wouldn't take my help and she could've used it. Branson had given her a similar bruise like the one on Kate's neck, and she had little money. I couldn't turn my back on her, and I fell for her, from the start. One thing led to another, we stayed together, me avoiding the family and bringing Russell on board to help us. She got pregnant, we got married then she left and went after him on her own." Will sighed. "And he killed her."

"I'm sorry, Will. Hang on," Richard said. "Pregnant?"

"Yes, you have a beautiful niece, Madelyn."

"Where is she?" he asked.

"Ireland, with the O'Keefes. We stayed in their B&B and became very close. They're like family. Isla, a retired MI6 agent Russell found through his Interpol mate, is nearby to make sure she stays safe."

"When did Ashlee die?" She cleared her throat.

"November last year."

"How old is Madelyn?" Her anger at Will subsided.

"She'll be a year next month."

"I don't blame you for thinking I worked for Branson. If I look so much like Ashlee—"

"You do." Will cut her off. "You were serious about the dream rubbish, then?"

"Afraid so."

"What did he say to you?" Will moved beside the bed.

"Before I knew him as a psychopath, we had a pleasant conversation. Then when he told me his last name..." She shuddered. "He mentioned you—Colin, I mean, and how Ashlee ran off with him and something about her being euphoric about it, his word choice was super creepy. Then we didn't really talk much because I was trying to stay alive."

"And I am sorry." Will squared his shoulders. "But you shouldn't have run off."

"I couldn't let you take me to the jerk."

"Don't blame me, you found him all on your own." Will straddled the chair next to the bed.

"Because you drove me there, look I don't want to argue with you, what do we do now?"

Will grinned. "There is no 'we.' I handle Branson, you leave."

Richard nodded. "As soon as possible."

"Where would you two prefer to go?" Will asked.

"She will be going to Paris. I will be helping you get Branson, turn him in."

"You keep saving lives, little brother. I'll be the one to kill him. And with your newfound shooting skills, I can't think of anyone better to protect her. You two go, this will be over soon."

She carefully pushed herself off of the bed. "He said he wasn't done with me, before he ran off. I think he'll find me no matter where I am." She thought to Will's baby girl. "Use me as bait."

"Are you mad? And I'm referring to both of you. Will, you can't kill the sociopath and, Kate, what do you mean use you as bait?" He scratched his head.

"I don't want to spend any time of my life running from the freak. So, to answer your question: no, I'm not crazy."

"Richard, I can and will kill Branson. Let's all get some rest. I'll decide my next move in the morning." Will directed his gaze at her. "Can I talk to you alone?"

What would he want to talk to her about? "Sure."

He narrowed his eyes at Will. "I'll give you five minutes."

When Richard was up the stairs and out the secret door, Will motioned for her to get in bed.

Slow and careful, she got back under the covers.

"Tell me." He fluffed her pillow then bent over her. "How much money will it take to get you to leave my brother alone?"

Chapter Eighteen
Near Death

"You're unreal."

"The background check on you, while you're clearly not working for Branson, there is something. It concerns me."

"What are you talking about?"

He sat on the edge of the bed. "Six months ago, you were in a car accident."

"Doesn't make me a criminal."

"Not at first glance. Did the car insurance not pay enough? Thought you'd come to England and bump into one of us Bennett's, get some of the family fortune?"

"What does my car accident have to do with anything? Go away." She shoved him as hard as her tender ribs would allow. "The uncontrollable urge to hit you is strong and I'm too tired and sore to do anything about it."

Will smirked. "Your car accident with the motorbikes. You're brilliant at the naïve and innocent act."

She lifted her water off the side table and removed the plastic lid off. Chewing on some pebble ice, she waited for accusatory Will to go on. "What are you suggesting now? I'm a Russian spy?" She paused. Wait a minute, motorcycle guys? Richard had a motorcycle. It couldn't be true. "You and Richard were in the accident?"

"Your acting skills never cease to amaze me."

She's had enough of his blame game. Jerking her water cup at him, she smiled as it soaked his face and shirt.

Will jumped up and glared at her.

"Don't point the finger at me. I came here to see

my dance teacher from Julliard. I had no idea about the accident."

Maybe why she dreamed about Richard? Some intuition deal about him being in the collision? Her heart raced in eager anticipation of maybe finally having an explanation for their déjà vu.

He wiped his face with a paper towel. "It's not a coincidence, it can't be. Tell me how much you want and be on your way."

She ignored how every inch of her ached and got up and moved toward him. Poking her finger against his chest, she backed him against the wall. "You ran into me, remember?"

"A little too convenient, wouldn't you agree?"

She wasn't a violent person, so why the urge to slap him? "You're an ass."

"Agreed." Richard walked in.

"We're done." She poked his chest one last time and fled to the bed.

"You tell him or I can. It's up to you, actress." Will walked out.

"Will could use a beating." She sank into the bed.

He laughed. "I know just what you mean. I get the urge to knock him around at least once a day. I brought you some soup. Russell made it."

"He accused me of coming here for your money."

"Come again?"

"Yes, says the car accident six months ago involved you two, and I wanted more money because I am greedy and dissatisfied with what the insurance paid me. He did a background check on me."

He sat beside her. "I heard you were a dancer."

"What?"

"The article. Well...what my parents told me about the story. Born and raised in Vegas and a dancer."

"Your names weren't mentioned. I didn't know who you guys were. Which means Will's theory is wrong."

"Yes, Russell conveniently convinced my parents to convince the media to keep hushed about our accident. It would have been bad publicity for Bennett Hotel and Crown Caroline; the two reckless thrill-seeking rich blokes. They referred to us as unidentified men whose safety depended on our anonymity. I think there's more to it, Will's obviously behind it."

"Richard." She thought on her conversation with Branson. "He was there."

"Who?"

"Branson, in Vegas on New Year's. Even at the same hotel my cousin's wedding was at, up at Mt. Charleston."

"That's why Will went to Vegas...makes sense now."

"Oh no." She remembered what she had told Branson. "I said your names, before I knew who he was. I'm sorry."

He caressed her hands. "No worries, you need to rest. And now we can take black magic and voodoo off of our list of why we have a connection."

"And reincarnation."

"I'm leaning more toward a near-death experience. We were both in comas."

"As crazy as it sounds, it's better than the alternatives, Richard." She squeezed his hands. "I didn't come here to take your money. To be honest, it makes me a little uncomfortable. I've never known any millionaires before."

"My father's the millionaire. Yes, he's shared his wealth with his sons, but a few indulgences aside, I'm quite well-rounded."

She smiled but stopped because her face hurt to make facial expressions.

"You should have some soup and get some sleep. I'll run to Judy's and get your things; tell her we're having a sleepover."

"She'll be thrilled," Kate said. "I'll call her and have her get a few things together for me. Seriously, what do I tell her?"

He reached in the pocket of his jeans and handed her his phone. "Tell her I'm whisking you off to Paris and not to pack too much. You can shop there. I'll think of something to tell her as to why I'm picking your things without you."

When she had finished her conversation with an elated Judy, she tossed Richard his phone. "Be careful."

Chapter Nineteen
A Change of Plans

Rest had eluded Will. He tossed and turned most of the night on Russell's couch. For a short amount of time, he knew sleep had come to him because he dreamt. Ashlee came to him, warning him but remaining untouchable as usual...he shook it off. Thinking about how he had lost the only woman he ever loved, would ever love, hurt too much to contemplate.

He would get Branson and end the psycho's life. Killing people who deserved it didn't bother him. No, he didn't enjoy killing anyone, but he had taken a life or two when necessary.

The innocence he saw in his daughter's eyes kept him pressing forward to get rid of Branson. Madelyn should never have to live like he and Ashlee had—not trusting anyone and paranoid. He wanted a normal and safe life for her. Ridding the world of one more evil devil like Branson settled right with him.

Kate was an impressive woman. Why he had accused her of coming after Richard's money, irritation and suspicion. She couldn't have known who they were. But what were the odds of her showing up like she had on the shore and getting into this mess? Seeing her had paralyzed him and shot the pain of losing Ashlee right through his every nerve ending all over again. The only thing he could have done at the time. walk off. He had hated her in the moment for haunting him and bringing the despair he'd buried deep down to the surface once more. Pretending had worked for him, until she showed up. Now, he wanted her. But he knew it was only because she mirrored Ashlee's image.

Rubbing his tired eyes and turning on his side, he lay in the dark and waited for sleep to take him once more.

***

Kate's eyes shot open. She woke startled and still in the mini ER at Russell's. A dim light glowed behind her.

She gazed around the room to find Richard asleep on a chair. As uncomfortable as he had to have been, his restful expression begged to differ. As a doctor, he must have found sleep in all kinds of places and unlikely positions. Seeing him beside her brought her instant Zen.

What about him did she find so comforting? Aside from his attractiveness, which she could honestly take in twenty-four hours a day, it had to be his tenderness. And not only in his words and smooth voice but his deeds. He showed her she mattered to him and somehow, she already knew it.

Her mind wandered to the possibility of a near-death experience. She had been in a coma for over a week after the accident. When she woke up, she had felt different, aware of something yet to be revealed. And a bright light and colorful kaleidoscope tunnel had flashed across her mind for a second. Had she spent time with him there? Why he had her every attention? Was she in love with him?

In sleep, he had a rumpled, boyish innocence she found endearing. She smiled over at him and sighed. Reaching for the water on the tray beside the bed, she cringed. The pain in her ribs suddenly hard to ignore.

He stood, stretching. "Can I get you anything?"

"My water." She moved her hand to her throat. Her voice sounded raspy but closer to normal.

He handed her the cup of water. "It's about time for more pain meds." He checked her IV bag and replaced it with a new bag of fluids.

"About to ask you." She sipped her water. "I tried to stay awake until you got back from Judy's, but I crashed. You don't think Branson will know I'm staying with them, do you?"

He yawned and covered his mouth, shaking his head. "No worries." He sipped a drink of water from his cup on the table beside the chair he had been sleeping on. "I think he's tending to his wound. I nailed his shoulder with a bullet. I was aiming for his heart but he moved."

"First time you've ever shot someone?"

He nodded. "Didn't like it, but I'd do it again." He fluffed the pillow behind her then sat on the bed. "Are you hungry?" He glanced at her throat and glowered.

"No, but would you bring me my bag?" She had Judy pack a thin scarf and needed to cover up the bruise. Whenever he eyed it, a murderous scowl crossed his face. Downplaying the visual reminder of Branson's attack would be better—out of sight and all that.

"Here you are." He lifted the bag off the floor and set it beside her.

After unzipping the bag, she pulled out a pink scarf, tied the soft fabric loosely around her neck, and smiled. "Better?"

He grinned. "A bit. I know it's still there, but not seeing it will keep my blood pressure down."

"Are you going to the hospital today?"

He shook his head. "Thanks for reminding me. I need to call and get another doctor to cover me." He reached in his pocket for his phone.

"What time is it?"

He pressed his phone to his ear and glanced at his watch. "About four a.m. Agnes, hello, this is Doctor

Bennett. I've had a family emergency and won't be able to make it in."

He listened to Agnes. What sort of family emergency had Agnes assumed? Dying parents or a seriously injured brother? No way could she imagine the scenario he found himself in, a murderer on their trail? And her to thank for it. Ultimately, she'd say it was all Will's fault, but there was no getting around the fact she had been the one to spill the beans about their names.

"Thanks, then. Yes, call if he can't make it." He ended the call and set his phone on the metal tray.

"Your hair." She reached out and touched it. "Shorter in my dreams or whatever those flashes were."

"I stopped cutting it after the accident." He toyed with a strand of her hair. "Yours was longer." He tucked it behind her ear then placed his hand tenderly on her bruised cheek. "How can I know you so well and yet not know anything about you?"

She placed her hand over his. "I'm assuming for the same reason I trust you without knowing why."

"I don't believe I have ever wanted to kiss any woman as badly as I want to kiss you." He leaned into her until his lips were over hers. "Once you're well, I plan on doing it often, if you're all right with it of course."

"I'm all right with it now."

When he pressed his lips against hers, the vision came. Lightning fast and clear as a sunny day. They were in front of a fireplace in each other's arms. The smell of him so like the ocean mixed with spices. Sea breeze, she called him. He laughed and called her cupcake.

The vision faded. He kissed her cheek, her jaw, and along the side of her neck. "Yes, like the memory...strawberry cupcakes," he whispered and grinned at her.

"Really?" She moved her hands to his face and felt over his one-day stubble. "I would have thought a flower maybe, not food."

He laughed. "It's dessert and happens to be my favorite."

She shrugged. "I guess it's okay, then."

"I'm sorry about your dance career."

"It's not your fault."

He fixed her scarf. "I'm afraid it is. I was careless."

"I drove through a panic attack, which means I'm stupid."

"Right, then, stupid and careless. We make quite a pair."

Quite a good pair, she thought and bit her lip.

"You're flight for Paris leaves at noon."

"What?" She frowned.

"I've arranged for my family's private jet to take you to Paris. You'll stay at the Bennett Hotel and will rest there until you're up for some sight-seeing. Hopefully Will and I will have taken care of Branson by then and I'll join you."

"No," she huffed.

"No to Paris, the hotel, sightseeing?"

"No thank you to all of it. I'm not going to run off and hide."

"It's you he wants. Will believes it will be like a hunt to him until he has you. Sociopaths like games apparently. And keeping you safe is my number one priority."

"I appreciate your concern for me, but I can help you get him. It's the only way."

"I agree." Will walked in the room.

"No, you don't." Richard looked away. "She goes where she'll be safe."

Will shook his head. "Plans have changed. Her safety is no longer a priority."

"What the hell are you talking about?"

Will's jaw clamped. "I got a phone call from Branson. He has Jack."

***

Jack spit the blood pooling in his mouth onto the concrete floor. His wrists were shackled over his head as he hung from a beam in the corner of a dark warehouse. He had come to after being beaten by two brutes.

His head throbbed and his right eye was swollen shut. He couldn't see out of it and shivered when a cool breeze blew over him and the water dripping over his head fell on his bare chest. Only wearing the shorts he had worn to bed, his body shivered, and he flinched when the demon named Hag hit him across the middle of his back with a leather strap for the second time.

Jack only had the energy to moan when Hag struck him again and again. Jack had lost count. The lacerations cutting into his skin like razorblades nauseated him.

"Not once." Jack paused. He tried to catch his breath wanting to say not once had he been questioned or asked to offer information about anything. Why the torture?

"What, boy?" Hag struck him again.

"What do you want from me?" Jack mumbled, almost a whisper.

"To rough you up a bit. Got to keep your big brother on the right path to bring Kate to us. The pictures we send him of you will help keep him motivated not to think twice on his word. Nothing personal." Hag dropped the strap and pulled a knife from his shirt pocket. Holding it up to Jack he grinned. "I know it doesn't seem like it could do much damage, but I'll let you decide."

Jack cried out in torment when Hag sliced the

knife across his chest.

"Sharp enough? Good." Frowning, he wiped the knife dripping with Jack's blood on a rag he pulled off a small table.

Jack searched for a distraction and studied the darkness in search for a way out. The moonlight showed dull and covered by clouds when Jack peered through the window to his left. There were no visible exits.

How was he going to get out of this mess?

The sound of footsteps outside the window caught his attention. A door open behind him, and his heart sped up.

A tall figure stepped in front of him and tipped his hat to Jack before blowing cigar smoke in his face. "Hello, boy. I see you've met Hag and Sykes. Try not to take this personal. It's your brother and Kate we're after. But until we get 'em, we're going to try a few new toys on you. Appreciate your sacrifice."

"Burn in hell," Jack mumbled.

The demented cowboy pressed his cigar into the deep gash across Jack's chest. "Cut him down and let him sleep before the next round."

Jack fell to his knees after Hag cut the ropes above his head.

"Tie him to the chair, Sykes." Branson walked off with a low chuckle.

Jack dry heaved and now shivered as he sat with his hands tied to the chair. He shifted to get comfortable, but his lacerated spine halted any movement. He dropped his head forward and contemplated a way to negotiate himself out of the dire predicament.

Chapter Twenty
Fed Up

Will briefed Richard and Kate on his bizarre phone encounter with Branson.

Will had been almost asleep when his phone rang. Richard eyeballed the number. Why had his brother Jack phoned him at nearly four in the morning?

"This better be important," Will said.

"I would never call unless it was, Will Bennett."

Jack's voice he did not hear. His stomach flipped. "Branson."

"You pretending to be Colin all this time is over. Thanks to Kate, I know who you really are and what a very privileged family you come from. I may have to give Jack here another beating for your deceit."

"Leave him out of this. It's me you want."

"It's the lady I want now, in exchange for your brother. I'd also like two million pounds."

"You are psychotic."

"I'm not your standard packaged guy."

"What you are is a lunatic. Why would I give her to you?"

"I'll kill your little brother if you don't. Now how would your mama and daddy take to you being responsible for them losing another kid? I read all about your baby sister Charlotte, poor thing died so young. And I can send my 'boys' over to your parents' right after I kill Jack."

"When?" Will had to get Jack away from the madman.

"I'll give you twenty-four hours, being a fair business man and all. We'll meet at the Cliffs of Moher, in Ireland at O'Brien's Tower at dawn. I have business in Ireland tonight and will take Jack along for the ride. I have some more lessons to teach him. But don't worry, I'll send you some pics, maybe a video or two, to help you keep the deal. You come with the woman and nobody else. Do I make myself clear?" He ended the call.

After Will finished filling them in, they stared at him, stunned.

"It's my fault." She pinched the bridge of her nose.

"It's Will's fault." Richard tugged at his shirt collar.

Will sighed. "Would you like an apology in writing?"

"You saying it might be enough for now."

Will glared at him. "Sorry. Happy now?"

"Surprisingly, no. You have to mean it. What do we do? And using her is not an option."

"He wants her for Jack, along with two million pounds."

"We can give it to him by shoving it down his throat."

"Take me, snipe him, and get your brother." She added herself into the Bennett brothers' discussion.

They both stared at her.

"You think it's that easy, do you?" Will scoffed.

"How would I know? I think we need to take action and with your brother involved now, I think using me *is* the only option."

Richard shook his head. "There has to be another way."

"Another way for what?" Russell asked when he walked in the room.

Will brought him up to speed.

Russell's brow crinkled, and he rubbed his hand across his chin. "I could phone Isla. She may know an independent agent we could hire to stand in as Kate. And I want to get some protection for your parents."

"Brilliant." Richard unclenched his fists.

Will rubbed his forehead. "Could work."

"Too risky." She massaged her temples. "He's not stupid and if Branson calls your bluff, he'll hog-tie you both, along with your brother."

"It will work." Will let out a harsh breath.

Richard drew nearer to her. "It's the only way."

"I'll phone Isla." Russell left the room.

Apparently, she was amongst the members of the royal family. No one told her what to do; they tried but didn't mean she had to listen. Okay, she might listen but wouldn't actually do what they asked, not if she didn't want to. Yes, she temporarily resided in Britain where people were subjects, but she as an American was about to wave her flag of free citizenship in all of their faces.

She stood and extended her arm with the IV in it to Richard. "Take it out."

He grinned at her. "Why?"

"Because I asked you to."

He did as she asked and secured a Band-Aid over the small needle prick.

"Where can I change?" She lifted her bag from the bed.

"Down the hall." Will pointed.

Every step radiated with pain, but she kept her posture as poised as she could manage.

Once she was in the bathroom, she dropped the bag and glanced at herself in the mirror. Fear seized her for an instant then transformed into a fireball of anger big enough to burn the place down. Now more than ever, she wanted to face the monster who'd done this to her. She loosened the scarf from around her neck and turned away from the mirror. Moving the handle in the shower, she knew she had to come up with a plan. Branson would kill Jack if she didn't show up; she knew it in her gut.

After she had cleaned up and changed into some comfortable attire, she slipped on her flats and secured the scarf around her neck. Makeup would be nice but a waste of her time; nothing could cover up the battered appearance she modeled.

Carefully she brushed her teeth. On closer inspection, she realized a trip to the dentist in order. One of her molars had been chipped from Branson's backhand. A quick dab of some lip gloss and she strolled out of the bathroom.

Her favorite doctor sat on the edge of the bed, sorting awkwardly through a pile of assault weapons.

"Any surgical instruments in there?" She mimicked his body language.

He rubbed his eyes. "I wish."

She picked up a dagger with "made for murder" written all over it. "I had a phase where I wanted to be a spy. I watched tons of Bond films. I had a thing for Roger Moore." She smiled. "Anyway, I researched and went to the shooting range when I wasn't dancing. Dancing became my passion which explains why the agent thing didn't last too long. This knife is the one for me. I'll take it tomorrow when we meet up with the cowboy."

"The only thing you'll be doing tomorrow"—he lifted the knife from her hand—"is recovering."

"I'm fed up with you and Will telling me what I should do."

He crossed his arms over his chest. "All right, Fed Up, what's your plan?"

"It's not Paris."

"Got it, what then?" He brushed her hair away from where it had fallen over her eyes. "I've done that before."

"Somehow, I know you have. Listen, using a stand-in for me is a bad idea, classic blunder done in way too many bad spy movies. I go, and once you have Jack, you two shoot Branson. I will be wearing whatever body armor you get me and we all watch the sunrise together."

"Huh." His brow creased. "Quite a fairy tale you've described. What about his 'boys' he mentioned to Will. Branson won't be alone. What do we do about them?"

"Use all the retired or still-active independent agents Russell knows to take them out."

"Aren't you afraid?"

"Who wouldn't be?"

"Then why are you willing to do this? You hardly know any of us. Well, excluding me. We seem to have a history we can't remember."

"Because it's the right thing to do, and I didn't survive the car crash to be stalked by some demented cowboy."

"For a small creature you're quite fierce."

"You have no idea." She tensed.

"I fear the wrath my next comment may trigger, so I'll put a little space between us." He pivoted away. "I forbid you going anywhere near the demented cowboy. We will get Jack without you."

"I spent some unwanted quality time with Branson and he's not playing with a full deck. The instant he realizes the stand-in isn't me, you're all dead. And I would like to get to know you better."

"Can't wait, but seeing what he's already done to you"—he threw his hands in the air and gestured to her battered appearance—"is precisely why you're not going."

"Who's going to stop me?"

He put his arms around her. "I will if I have to."

"I can do this."

"'Course you can, but I don't want you to."

"Why?"

"You may want to sit for this, I know I should." He altered her scarf after they sat on the edge of the bed. "I know this is going to sound mad. I'm quite certain, and I can't remember how it happened, not yet, but…"

He paused.

"What?"

"I know very little about you, but what I do know from all of the little things is, I was most definitely in love with you."

Chapter Twenty-One
Dreams Come True

"Wow." It was all she could whisper out.

"The worst delivery ever, no doubt, and I've made you cry. I should have written a poem." He bowed his head.

Her eyes misted up, didn't happen to her often. "I don't cry. I'm touched. You write poetry?"

"No."

"You should, and deep down I'm pretty sure...I was in love with you, too."

"Wow."

"I'm coming with you."

He put his arms around her and pressed his forehead to hers. "Afraid not."

"I'll still do it, even if you don't agree."

"I don't doubt it." He led her up the stairs and into Russell's bedroom. "You said you trusted me earlier, I'm asking you to trust me now."

"Okay."

His eyes roamed to the open bedroom door. "There's something else I need to tell you." He paused. "Not here." He kissed her forehead. When they ended up downstairs and in front of the room Will had held her in, he switched the light on and they stepped inside.

"For months I've dreamt of you. I could never see your face. You were always out of my reach, but I heard your voice, calling to me. You spooked yet?" He leaned against the wall.

She raised her chin. "No. I had the same dreams of you. Only I stayed behind you, calling to you. You couldn't hear me. I never said your name, but I asked you to stop, to wait for me."

"I asked you the same thing and now you're here.

It's both the strangest and best thing to ever happen to me." He lowered his head. "I've also had some different dreams—nightmares apart from the one where Branson attacked you at Pendennis. Seeing how my dreams and yours are a possibility of the past and my nightmare dreams seem to be of future events is why I can't let you go. If what I've seen has any truth to it, what happens at The Cliffs of Moher is a bloody mess."

She rubbed her shoulder. "I don't need your permission. What did you see?"

"I can't go spouting these dreams off to you or Will because he'll think I'm mad and try to stop me from helping Jack. And somehow, I know you and your strong will, you'll try to plot some other way with you still being involved." He kissed her, gentle yet firm and urgent. "I want us to have a chance to remember our mysterious past together and the chance to fall in love again. I'd rather spend the rest of my life begging your forgiveness for what I'm about to do than putting flowers on your grave."

He had rushed out the door and locked it before she knew what hit her. And it was the sweetest most wonderful thing anyone had ever spoken to her.

She didn't scream at him through the door or bang on it, it would have hurt too much. Didn't mean she wasn't pissed off, livid, incensed, and gnashing-her-teeth mad.

It seemed he proved as stubborn as she. A trait she would normally admire in a man, but seeing as he had trapped her in the cell block, she found it annoying.

Pacing the floor and cursing his blessed name, she finally sat on the lone chair in the center of the room. A plan would come to her, and she hoped it would be soon because her stomach growled.

In what felt like a few hours later, the door

opened.

"Ready for some breakfast?" Russell smiled.

She followed him up the stairs and into the kitchen. A large selection of fruit and pastries covered the table.

She snatched some grapes and a croissant and sat. "They left?"

Russell nodded. "Your flight leaves at noon."

"I told Richard I wasn't going to Paris."

"You're not." He handed her a hot cup of tea. "He thought you might enjoy Spain."

"I don't speak Spanish."

"Valdes does—he's the Interpol friend doing me a favor and will be taking over my watch over you in Barcelona. I'm meeting up with Will and Richard in Ireland."

She scanned the room for the time and found the kitchen clock. She only had a few hours to figure out how to escape her watchdog.

"How did you get involved in this mess? You're Australian, right?" she asked between bites of the croissant.

"I am, but I moved to the UK to work. I had a mess of my own years ago. Resembles Will's nightmare."

"I don't understand, but I'd like to if you'll share." She reached for a spoon and bowl before getting some melon.

"It drives you crazy not knowing things, doesn't it?" He walked to his bedroom and returned with a small photo album. "Here."

She wiped her hands on a napkin then opened the gray-leather binder. Inside lay a photo of a younger version of Russell and his beautiful bride.

"You were married?"

"Happily."

"The secret-spy life not for her?"

He shook his head. "Elena never would have approved of my methods."

She stopped on the page with the photo of a baby girl swaddled in a pink fuzzy blanket.

"Nicole," Russell whispered. "A few months old there."

"Adorable and has her mother's big brown eyes. Where are they now?" She flipped to the next few pages, revealing what appeared to be a toddler-sized Nicole.

"The cemetery." He lifted the book from her.

Her heart stopped. "I'm sorry. How?"

"They were murdered in our home. I was gone, found them when I returned. You see"—he cleared his throat—"I understand the anger, it comes after the agony and despair of such an unimaginable tragedy. I know what Will's going through. The hate can be consuming if you let it. I did and will pay for it at judgment day."

"You killed the person responsible?"

"Yes."

"Feel better?"

"Not anymore. Richard knows what I went through, apart from the revenge part. He thinks you're more than capable and trusts you. It's Branson he doesn't trust. I would have locked you in the room as well."

What Richard meant about flowers on her grave, it was because of Russell's sad loss. "Did you get the stand-in for me?"

"I'll pick her up this evening."

"Are you flying first class?"

"I'll fly my own plane, thank you. I've never been a fan of commercial flights."

"Dublin, was it?" She had no idea where the Cliffs of Moher were in Ireland. She'd have to Google it.

"You won't get any information from me. Nice try

though."

She bit a nail. Her plan had to be executed now or never. She contemplated what little white lie to spew.

"Something wrong?" Russell started clearing the food from the table.

"My earrings. I lost them."

"You can buy new ones or Richard can get them for you. His father does own the largest jewelry chain in the world."

"I don't want new ones. These are special."

"When did you last have them?"

"I think I left them in the cell block." She slowly got up and exaggerated the pain. When she gripped her side and hobbled toward the stairs, Russell stopped her.

"Easy, I'll check for you."

When he made it down the stairs, she grabbed a quart bottle of orange juice from the counter, along with a bag of bagels. Following as quietly after him as she could, she made sure he was searching for the earrings she never had, set the juice and bagels down on the floor inside the cell block, and shut and locked the door.

"Don't do this, Kate!" Russell shouted at her through the door, pounding furiously. She steeled herself and walked away. He wouldn't starve to death before someone released him.

In the kitchen, she found his cell phone on the counter. She snatched it and hurried to Russell's bedroom and down to the mini ER. Once she had gathered her bag, which had two of Richard's credit cards in it and a blonde bob wig, some rope and a few knives added to the mix, she hunted for the weapons he had been going through on the bed. After twenty minutes and no luck, she went into Russell's room. Bingo. She smiled at the black duffel bag full of guns and weapons on his bed.

After she mapped the directions to the airport on the phone, she drove comfortably in his Porsche and tightened her grip over the steering wheel. She'd never driven such a luxury vehicle or driven on the wrong side of the street. It felt wrong anyway. Russell's phone rang.

"Russell's phone," she said.

"May I speak to Mr. Hamilton?"

"He's got food poisoning"—the first thing to spring to her mind. "Can I help you?" *Way to be on point, Adams.*

"This is the pilot, James. Shall I cancel the flight plans for him and Ms. Adams, then?"

"No, this is Ms. Adams, I'll still be going but not to Spain. Could you make it Ireland?"

"Not a problem, miss. Dr. Bennett asked me to oblige you. Dublin or Shannon?"

"How kind of Dr. Bennett." She'd add it to why she should forgive him for locking her up. "Can I let you know when I arrive?"

"Of course, see you then, Ms. Adams."

"Thank you, and please keep this between us." She tossed the phone in the passenger seat.

Was she crazy? Going into the presence of a devil like Branson made her closer to psychotic.

Russell's phone squawked again.

"Yes."

"I may have the wrong number," a woman spoke.

"Russell's got a bad case of food poisoning, came on quick. Can I help you?"

"Did you know if he still needed my services in Shannon?"

So, she would be flying to Shannon, Ireland. "Are you the stand-in?"

"I am."

"There's been a change in plans but I could use your help."

"Decided to do it yourself?"

"Yep."

"Not a good idea. I'll contact Russell when I arrive this evening."

She turned off the phone, wanting to save the battery. She'd forgotten to search for Russell's charger before she left.

Her mind wandered to Jack. She hoped he would survive. Who knew what Branson could be doing to him? Yes, she hardly knew him but from their brief encounter on the beach, he appeared a decent man and undeserving of the hell he most likely dwelled in.

And Richard... He'd be upset with her once he found out she'd left Russell locked up and followed him. Maybe she'd text him when she arrived in Ireland.

Chapter Twenty-Two
Alias

What to say? She had no clue.

Resting comfortably at the Oak Wood Arms Hotel near the airport in Shannon—thanks to James the pilot—she charged Russell's phone on the charger James had given her.

He assured her Dr. Bennett would insist she take it and he could get a new one.

She'd had a late lunch and reluctantly popped a pain pill just before the phone rang. She checked the caller ID. Richard. Answering would only tip him off to her solo spy mission, so she ignored it. As much as she wanted to hear his pleasant voice, it wasn't a good idea.

She drew open the curtains and peered cautiously around the grounds. The phone dinging, alerting her to a text message, so she sat on the bed and snatched it from the table.

Richard: *Where the bloody hell is Kate? Valdes phoned Will, she never arrived!!!*

She frowned. "I forgot about the guy in Spain."

She had to get in the voice of Aussie Russell. *Hmmm. Here goes nothing.*

Russell: *Crikey, she's fine. You know how stubborn the woman is. Wanted me to stay with her. I have her convinced she's formulating a plan.*

Richard: *Good, keep her safe. Get her to Valdes soon. We'll see you tonight.*

Russell: *What time?*

Richard: *Seven, in the lobby at the Oakwood Arms Hotel. It's close to the airport.*

Russell: *You there now?*

Richard: *Yes, ask Kate to call me.*

Russell: *Fat chance.*

Richard: *True, but give her the phone. I'll call now.*

No! He couldn't call her. She would cave at the sound of his voice.

The phone rang. But not hearing his voice would be worse.

Be strong, Kate.

On the third ring, she accepted the call. "Guilt-ridden I hope?"

He laughed. "Beside myself. I can hardly function. I hear you've changed my plans for you."

"Not surprised, are you?" Where was his room? "How's Ireland?"

"Lovely, wish you were here."

"Liar."

"You should stop formulating your own plans. I can almost hear your mind swimming with all sorts of scenarios."

"You should have taken me with you." In the room next to hers, a door shut. She set her other ear to the wall.

"Let me speak to Russell."

"He's busy." She swore Richard was in the next room. Good thing she had registered under Austina Powers and paid with the last of the cash she had. "Hello?"

"Still here. Why is Russell so busy?"

He seemed suspicious. "Food poisoning. He's been in the bathroom all morning."

"Hang on, love," he said, with Will in the background telling him something. "It turns out Russell sprang from the cell you locked him in and explained the situation to Will. Our pilot informed him you've arrived in Shannon. What was that, Will?"

She rolled her eyes.

"Will says an Austina Powers has checked in here."

Why had she blurted such a ridiculous cover name? It popped out before she could change it.

A knock at the door startled her. "Let me in, Ms. Powers."

She ended the call, Richard still knocking at the door. From the black bag, she pulled out the blonde wig, pulled it on, and grabbed her things before opening the window and painfully wriggled outside. Her ribs were a little better from the pain meds but not much.

Once she was down the road in a cab, she called him.

"Missed me."

"You went out the window, didn't you?"

"Yes, and I would appreciate it if you'd let me be."

"Afraid I can't."

"I know this is crazy, but I miss you." She bit her lip.

"I miss you more."

"I have to figure out a way to save your brother."

"My job. Stay clear of the cliffs, Ms. Powers."

"I don't make promises I can't keep. Hanging up now." She turned off the phone.

The draw to him was like some unseen gravitational force. For a split second, she considered asking the cab driver to turn around, but she would only regret it. Richard would have her locked up somewhere else.

"Where to, lass?" the driver asked.

"I need a hotel near the Cliffs of Moher."

"Cliffs of Moher Hotel all right?"

"Yes." She straightened the wig then put her sunglasses on. What name should she register under this time?

***

"Enjoy your stay, Ms. Nikita." The hotel clerk adjusted the lapels of her jacket.

She smiled and followed the bellman to her room on the main floor. She wanted an easy escape route in case Richard found her again. Her thoughts wandered to Branson, who could be close. And what the hell was she doing, playing 007? She sighed and then thanked the bellman and shut the door. After dropping her bags on the bed, she paused to turn the phone on. No voicemail or texts from him left her disappointed, but, with any luck, that meant he'd realized it best to let her do her thing.

Too bad she had to pay for the room on credit card. Cash would better ensure her secrecy from Richard. Hopefully, he wouldn't be alerted by his card company.

A short nap and a long and hot shower later, she changed into some thin black sweats and dried her hair. Lip gloss was all the effort she could muster to help her pale glow.

She turned on the TV. Some serious drama played across the screen, but she paid scant attention. She needed the noise to fill the silence. She needed a plan.

The phone rang, and she jumped then rushed to load the first of four guns.

"I wondered when I'd hear from you." She turned off the television.

"Let me in, Ms. Nikita." He chuckled.

She opened the curtains, ready to flee, only to discover Richard standing in front of the window. His handsome face showed an expression somewhere between happy and frustrated.

She smiled at him. "I'll go out the door this time."

"Will's waiting there with chloroform. It's him or me you battle, you choose." He winked.

She threw the phone on the bed and peered

through the peephole, her eye focused on a bored and frustrated Will.

Returning to the window, she opened the sash for him.

He climbed in and secured the latch before closing the curtains. Holding his phone to his ear, he grinned. "I'm in, thanks for standing guard." He put his phone in his pocket and scowled at her. "Do you have any idea how careless this is? Branson could be nearby."

"I wore the wig in and haven't left the room."

"I thought you trusted me."

She turned away from him and picked up one of the guns. "Hasn't changed. Your brother's with Branson because of me and my big mouth."

He turned her to face him then removed the gun from her before tossing it on the bed. "I happen to like your big mouth." He stared at her lips. "This is Will's mess we're tangled in and I'm not blaming you so you shouldn't, either. You're doing too much after what you've been through."

She shrugged.

"Come on." He carefully placed her on the bed and sat beside her. "Branson phoned Will again, sent some unpleasant photos of Jack."

"All the more reason to take me."

He leaned forward and rubbed his eyes. "Jack and I are fine, in my dream, we make it."

"Will?"

"I'd rather not discuss it, it's awful."

"Me?"

"It's unclear. You're hurt and it's enough to make sure you keep away from this rubbish."

"Then Will shouldn't go, I'll be fine, trust me." But would she?

He straightened. "You I trust, it's Branson I have my doubts about. And have you met Will? I can't stop him or you it seems." He carefully placed the guns beside the bed on the floor and laid back. "What Jack's being put through is killing me. Having you involved only makes it worse."

She lay beside him and stared at the ceiling. "I should be more upset with you for locking me up. But I'm worried about you and would rather do this together."

He propped himself up on his elbow. "Branson killed Will's wife, he nearly killed you, and he's using Jack as a punching bag. Anything we do together will be after I take care of him."

"There you go, bossing me around, telling me what and when to do things. Are you the Lone Ranger now?"

"Best outcome, yes."

"You'd kill Branson?'

He brushed his knuckles over her cheek. "I want to kill him but would settle for giving him a good beating before turning him in. But first things first, let's take you to Russell's and put you and Will in the cell block."

"Good luck. How are you going to get Will to comply?"

"Chloroform, rope, and perhaps strong medication to keep him asleep." He grinned.

"And me?"

"I'm hoping you'll see things my way, love."

"And if I don't?"

"I will do what is necessary to see you make it through this alive."

She drank in his electric-blue eyes, but the worried expression he gave her almost stopped her heart. He had given her a similar stare in another place in time.

The image of her losing him flickered and burned out. It made her body sting.

She stroked his cheek. *Kiss me.*

He didn't hesitate.

When his lips met hers, their bond connected and solidified their forgotten history. As the kiss deepened, a vision from a past life came, flirting around the edges of her memory. They were dressed in Victorian attire and stood behind a waterfall. He spoke in full medical mode and she told him she loved him. When he admitted the same, they kissed for an eternity until all of the feelings sweeping over her severed in an abrupt and harsh manner. He ceased to exist.

Inside, she felt the agony of losing him again and pulled him closer, now confused, she held him tighter. "You left."

"Against my will. Being torn from you was no spring day. I must have woken before you—near-death experience perhaps."

Would they ever unravel the mystery? Did it matter?

"I'm crushing you." When he went to lift himself off of her, she held him tighter. What had crushed her was standing alone by the waterfall. If an image from a dream registered so painful, what would losing him now do to her? Her mind spiraled as heavy dark clouds attacked her senses. The finality of losing him suffocated her and transported her in time to the desolate loss of her dad.

And losing Richard could definitely happen with his mind set and fixed on going after Branson. She searched his eyes and in them found the only place with comfort. How could she explain the profound impression he'd made on her in days? He had never been a stranger to her, even when she first met him on the beach, she knew him somehow. The room grew darker as the sun set and the modest light coming in through the curtains faded, but somehow, she felt rays of light around them.

"I," she whispered, *need you now.*

He knew, without her uttering a sound, his expression showing understanding. His lips found the soft flesh of her bruised neck where he planted a gentle warm kiss. Then he moved his mouth to her ear. "I need you more but don't want to hurt you."

As badly as her body ached from the deep bruises Branson had put on her, Richard not touching her was worse. *Then don't stop.*

He acted on her thoughts as if she'd spoken them aloud. First, he conquered her lips with his and no doubt would have carried her away to a perfect place only he could take her had Will not started banging on the door.

"I should have killed him last night." He grinned at her.

"Let me help you drug him, but I stay with you."

"Take this." He reached into his pocket and handed her a small glass vile. "Slip half of this into his drink if the opportunity arises. It will knock him out for a short while." He kissed her tenderly before standing up.

Chapter Twenty-Three
No Time to Be Nice

She rolled her eyes at the bantering coming from Richard and Will in her room. She had hurried to the bathroom before he let Will in. She was a little disheveled after her time with him, time she couldn't stop smiling about. Once she had her scarf in place over Branson's handprint and some makeup over her bruised face, she walked into the room.

"You can't expect me to hand my wife's murderer over to you and sit and wait for you to take him out. Branson is my kill." Will scowled.

"You're in way over your head here, Will. You're talking about killing someone. Think of your daughter. If something were to happen to you—"

"She'd have you."

Richard threw his hands up. "Kate, you try talking some sense into him. I need some air." He walked out of the room.

It was her turn to try and simmer Will down.

"I'm hungry." She grabbed her room key off the table. "Let's go eat."

"Hang on." Will blocked the door. "Best we have Richard pick something up. I'm sure Branson's not far from here."

"Okay."

Will brought his phone to his ear. "We're hungry, bring us some food." He dropped his phone in his jacket pocket.

"You could have been nicer about it."

"I don't have time to be nice."

She noticed his usual avoidance of eye contact with her. It must be miserable for him, considering how closely she resembled his lost love. "I'm sorry."

When she stepped in front of him, he attempted to

move away from her.

"Sorry."

"For reminding you of Ashlee? I don't blame you for avoiding me."

He nodded.

"Does your daughter look like her?"

The hard lines of his face softened. The smile the mention of his daughter brought to his lips shined bright.

"Exactly, but she has my eyes and hair color. Here." He reached in his jacket and pulled out a crumpled picture. "It's a bit worn."

She accepted the picture he offered. Will, Ashlee, and their baby. They were standing in a green field, unaware they were caught in someone's camera lens.

"Mr. O'Keefe takes pictures on his daily walk."

"Your family's so beautiful. I can see we could be twins. *My being here, looking like her… I'm haunting him.*

He sat beside her on the bed. "At first glance, yes. But there was something indefinable about her, something deeper than looks."

"You, this is the you she brought out." She studied his serene expression in the picture and how he held their baby in his strong arms.

"What do you mean?" He snatched the picture from her.

"I've only ever seen you irritated; I like the Will in the picture better."

He tucked the picture in his jacket.

"Russell told me about his wife and daughter. He got his revenge and doesn't seem okay about it. Do you really think killing the cowboy is going to make you feel better?"

"I know it won't, but my daughter will be safe and so will my family. We're all better off when he's dead."

"Do you really think he'll try to kill me?"

"Eventually, yes, but for now, he wants to control you." He gripped her arms and made uneasy eye contact. "The other night when I drove you to Pendennis, I never would have turned you over to him."

"But you said—"

"I lied."

She could see what Ashlee must have fallen in love with. Will's harsh exterior proved a facade to cover up the good man beneath.

"Would have been nice to know before I assaulted you with my heels."

Will grinned. "Caught me completely off guard with."

"You don't show hurt now. Is it getting easier to see me?"

"A bit. While I'm apologizing, I should have helped you on the shore, when I knocked you down. Normally I would have, it's, I was stunned by your resemblance to Ashlee."

"It's okay." She smiled. "What will you do? When this is over, I mean."

"I'll move home with my baby girl, by the O'Keefes."

"Not near your family?"

"My parents and I don't really get along, and I don't want to run my father's businesses. He'll bother me about it if I'm too close, and my mum will push me to marry someone."

"Why don't you get along with your parents? Do you think you ever will get married again?"

"You're quite nosy."

She nodded.

"It's complicated with my parents, but no, I won't marry again."

"How can you be sure?"

"Why does my love life interest you?"

217

"You shouldn't be alone and your baby will need a mom. I think you'll remarry."

He drew nearer. "Perhaps if you fall out of love with Richard, I will."

She opened her mouth to speak but nothing came, empty of thought and speech.

"I knew it would shut you up."

"You're joking, ha ha."

"Maybe. At first, I'd be with you because you reminded me of Ashlee, but your eyes would remind me you weren't her. Then I might fall for you. You of course would fall in love with me and twist my arm into marrying you."

She laughed. "Some scenario."

"Admit it." Will smirked. "If you hadn't fallen for Richard, you'd have fallen for me."

"You're delusional." He always seemed to know how to irk her. And she hated him, partly because he was right. If she didn't love Richard with all of her heart, she might be strangely drawn to Will in some out-of-her-mind-attracted-to-the-bad-boy phase. "No." She stood and glared down at him. "We would never work. I'm too easily pushed to violence at your every word. I'd end up in jail for abusing you."

He stood in front of her. "You're probably right. Best I accept defeat now. Richard's smitten. It's gross really."

"You're jealous." She nudged him.

"Why would I be jealous? He's going to have his hands full with you. I'll enjoy watching his frustration at the hands of such a small woman."

"I think I have a pair of heels in my bag. Don't make me use them."

"Friends, then?" He extended his hand to her.

She accepted his hand. "Friends."

This only made it harder to help Richard keep Will from The Cliffs of Moher. Shouldn't Will have a chance to get his revenge? Confused and caught up in nonsensical reasoning had her seeing things his way. But if it saved his life and kept him around for his baby, then she'd do it.

Will's phone alerted him to a text. His face went white.

"What?" she asked.

"It's from Branson. A video of Jack."

"Maybe we should wait for Richard."

Will touched the screen on his phone.

She reluctantly watched Branson break Jack's arm with a long piece of metal in some old shed or small warehouse. Jack moaned and appeared to have been tortured for hours. His right eye was swollen shut, and the rest of his body tattooed in scrapes and deep cuts along every inch of his bare chest and spine.

She covered her hand over her mouth at the nausea. Will started throwing hotel objects around the room. He punched the wall and blurted expletives.

She held Will by the arms and tried to settle him down. "We'll get him. Sit." She somehow convinced him. Remembering the glass vile Richard had given her, she walked to her bag where she'd tucked it away for safekeeping. Now was her chance to offer him a drink to calm him down—and drug him and tie him up.

When had she turned into a person who tied someone else up?

Chapter Twenty-Four
In a Bind

Quite proud of herself, she grinned. Who knew she had a talent for the spy life? Once she had slipped the drug in his tea, she sat behind Will on the bed and started massaging his shoulders. She talked him down to an almost-calm mood before he mumbled something about her needing to learn how to make a proper cup of tea. Then she tied him to the bed and finished the last knot on his wrist, he started coming to. And where was Richard? Getting food shouldn't take so long.

Thankfully, her dad had schooled her in tying knots on their summer trips to their cabin in Colorado. So, she knew the rope would hold him but was more concerned about his lousy attitude when he woke.

A weak smile tugged at his lips and a low muffled laughter started.

Hmmm. Not the response I expected. "Payback's funny to you?"

He cleared his throat. "If you wanted me in bed, all you had to do was ask."

"You're delusional."

"I thought we were friends," Will mumbled, on a more serious note.

"We are, and friends don't let friends go after crazy people and get killed."

"I have to be there. Branson said I had to bring you and come alone. We can't risk Jack's life."

She pressed her fingers to her lips.

"Kate, I can take Sheridan instead of you, but I have to be the one to do this. It's my battle not yours or Richard's. Tell me, what's your plan?"

"I can't because I don't know but it will be better this way, trust me. Want to watch TV?" She snatched the remote off the nightstand and channel surfed until she found some car show.

"What I want is for you to untie me and run because when I get my hands on you—"

"You'll what? Chloroform me again?"

"No, I'll kiss you then I'll figure out a way to keep you out of my way."

"Kiss me? I'm not Ashlee." Maybe the drug she gave him had a weird side effect.

"So?"

"You really are a jerk."

"Sometimes I am. Doesn't change the fact I still want to kiss you."

She sat next to him. "Are you crazy? I'm in love with Richard, who happens to be your brother."

"There's something only a kiss from you can tell me."

"I can't believe we're actually having this conversation. What, pray tell, do you believe kissing me will reveal?"

"Untie me and find out." He smirked.

"Not happening."

They both turned to the door; Richard walked in with his arms full of bags of food. The big grin spread across his mouth made her heart skip a beat.

"How did you manage this? You are the most extraordinary woman I've ever met."

Will scoffed.

"Apparently, it's what I do." She straightened. "Super fun. Especially when he came to and thought I tied him up for a romp in the sack." She stopped laughing when her eyes caught Will's glare.

He snickered then cleared his throat. "Right, then. Hungry, Will?"

"Whatever you're up to, it won't work, and when I get out of the ropes, I'm whipping you with them." Will glared at her.

"I should put you out of your misery. I'd be humiliated, too, mate." He handed off a sub sandwich to her.

"Thanks." She took a bite. "Tying him up drained me."

He leaned down and kissed her forehead. "I meant it. I'm impressed."

"It was only because I was distracted with worry," Will said. "Branson sent a video of him breaking Jack's arm. Cut me loose so I can kill the bastard!"

"Broke his arm?" He narrowed his eyes. "I'll kill the lunatic!"

She touched his arm. "We'll get him."

He nodded and, after taking a few deep breaths, held the sandwich up to Will's mouth.

"I'll get out of this, and when I do, I swear your girlfriend is not going to know what hit her."

He shoved part of the sandwich in Will's mouth. "He called you my girlfriend. I quite like the sound."

Will bit Richard's finger.

"Ouch! I've had about enough of your tantrum, Brother." He pulled a small syringe from his pocket and snapped off the lid, revealing a small long needle.

"I will never forgive you if you do this," Will seethed through his teeth.

"Then you'll hate me the rest of our lives." He pulled Will's jacket down enough to see the skin of his arm and stuck the needle in.

"We're only half-brothers anyway, so hating you won't be..." Will shook his head as the shot took effect.

"Hating me won't be what? And what do you mean we're half-brothers?" He smacked Will's face to keep him awake.

"Ask Mum and Dad. They'll tell you who my father rea..." Will's head fell forward.

"He made it up," she assured Richard. He stood

stiff, stunned by Will's comment.

"I'm not so sure. It's low, even for him. Doesn't matter, I'll worry about it later. However, Ms. Nikita, while I do appreciate your help with Will, I'm afraid I can't let you come along, either."

"What are you going to do, Dr. Jekyll? Stab me with some sleep drug, too? Do you always carry around syringes?" She put her fisted hands on her hips.

"Not generally. This was a first. I'm going to ask you to let me handle this and you stay here with Will."

"Thanks for asking, but no. I will be coming with you."

He held her gently in his arms then caressed her face. "Then you leave me no choice." He kissed her, and her senses drank in all of him, and as his hands roamed to her lower back and under her shirt, she wasn't complaining...until the needle pricked the top of her bottom.

She jerked away. "How could you?" Her head grew heavy, and she blinked rapidly, trying to keep her eyes open.

He placed his hands on her arms. "Go on and be angry at me, we'll work it out once this is over."

"And if something happens to you?"

"Nothing is going to happen to me."

The room tunneled then she met darkness.

***

He frowned at her and Will, passed out and beside one another on the bed. He put a pillow between them, not liking how near they appeared, then checked the rope around her ankles and wrists.

He sat beside her. What would she do to him when she woke up? He'd have to be sure to keep chloroform out of her small reach. In his eyes, she truly was the most beautiful woman he'd ever seen. He carefully brushed away the hair from her cheek before Will started to snore.

224

Surely, she would be fuming at him, but he reminded himself it would all be worth it when his brothers and the woman he knew he loved were safe. All of this would be over soon. He would wait for Russell to arrive. He needed him to make his mission successful. With Russell and Kate's stand-in to aid him, getting Jack back alive would work, and killing Branson would free his family of any more harm.

Will would surely never forgive him for not letting him avenge his wife, but he'd live with it. Seeing Will die in his dream hurt him more deeply than he ever would have thought. He loved his jerk of a brother even though they hadn't gotten along in years. And it might take years to repair their relationship, but that was a much better option than the alternative. And his dreams were more premonitions as of late, so he wouldn't risk losing Will.

He moved to the chair and closed his eyes. He needed to get what rest he could. Dawn would approach in hours, whether he was ready or not.

***

"This isn't going well at all," Charlotte whispered to Ashlee during choir practice.

"What's the latest?" Ashlee scanned the paper Charlotte handed her. "Now Richard's the one in trouble? Charlotte, I'm sorry. I never meant for this to happen. And I never saw a scenario where Jack got tangled up in this."

"It's not your fault. I'm the one meddling. Richard believes he'll live if he goes alone because of the scenario he's been dreaming about. I'm starting to think a ghost appearance is inevitable."

Ashlee shook her head. "But you can't. Perry banned you from ghost appearances after you were moved off the angel list. Have you checked the schedule for deaths tomorrow morning?"

"No, but a good idea. I'll get on it straightaway." Charlotte slowly rose from her seat.

Ashlee pulled her arm. "Here comes Henry."

Charlotte drank in the sight of her husband, and she kissed his cheek after he occupied the seat beside her. "What brings you here?"

He frowned. "I'll tell you after the singing's over."

Charlotte shrugged at Ashlee. After two long songs, they rose and walked out of the great hall.

"I'll be at Heaven's Gate. Let me know what he says." Ashlee left.

Charlotte sized up her towering husband. "Spill it."

"You're not going to like what I have to say."

"Tell me anyway."

"Your meddling is the problem, lass. Sometimes, no matter what you do, the outcome can't be changed or, as is always the case with you, it's made worse." He held her by the arms gently and kissed her forehead as he always did when he was about to deliver bad news. "Will isn't the only one dying tomorrow. Richard and Jack will be arriving, too."

Chapter Twenty-Five
Revelation from a Kiss

Kate hovered in the best dream. The sweetest kiss brushed over her lips, subtle and warm before her tied hands moved over Richard's head and rested around his neck. Darkness filled the room. Something out of the ordinary about his kiss gave her pause. There was nothing wrong with it, nothing at all. But when it occurred to her the lips she kissed and the fresh cedar cologne she inhaled weren't Richard's but Will's, her eyes popped open and she rolled off of him and started beating his chest with her tied fists. The pain in her ribs stopped her.

Will laughed then started coughing.

"I hate you," she screamed.

"Because I kissed you or because you enjoyed it?"

"You're so full of yourself. I was half asleep and thought you were Richard." She rested her head on the pillow between them.

"Tell yourself whatever you need to and get the knife out of my left pocket, would you, love?"

She sat up and glared at him. "You trust me with a knife after what you did?" She awkwardly pulled the knife out of his pocket. "I'll cut through your rope if you promise to take me with you."

Will frowned. "You know I'll say anything to get you to do it because I have to kill Branson."

"What if he kills you?"

"Then it will be for a good cause."

"I think you should be the one to capture him then turn him in. And you know Branson isn't going to buy the body double. Take me with you, or you and I watch the sunrise from bed."

"Doesn't sound so bad."

She tried to cut her own rope.

Will sighed. "All right, then, cut me loose and I'll do the same for you. I'll let you come because I happen to agree with you. He'll kill Jack once he sees you're not there."

She moved slowly to her knees and over Will. She sawed clumsily through the thick knot she'd made around his wrists. "This may take a while."

"We don't have a while."

"Did you guys get the money Branson wanted?"

"Most of it, but he'll be dead before he gets a chance to count it."

"Did you get what you wanted from our kiss?"

He nodded up at her while she still cut through the rope.

"Well, tell me what kissing me revealed There." She freed his hands, and he pushed her aside and bent over to untie his feet.

Once loose, he stood and stretched. She cleared her throat.

"All right, what I know from kissing you"—he pulled her in his arms and held on to her tight—"is as lovely as it was, I'm still in love with my wife and my attraction to you has everything to do with her."

"You're a good man, Will Bennett. Forget what I said about hating you."

He shrugged. "My good side has limits, which is why you're going to stay here."

"I should have known better than to trust you." Exhaustion, the only explanation she could think of for her not seeing this coming.

"I have this brotherly urge to protect you, which is a first for me. I usually don't have brotherly feelings for beautiful women, if you know what I mean." He dropped her on the bed. "I'll get my things in my room and check on you before I head to the cliffs."

He turned on the lamp and searched around the room for weapons—the guns that had been there, gone. "Don't run off." Will winked and left with her room key.

Now, she had time to think and her every molecule fumed at Richard's doing. Once she got to him and confirmed his safety, it would take a miracle to save him from the wrath of her anger.

The digital clock in the room flashed three forty-five which meant the sun would rise in over an hour. How would she get out of this mess and to the cliffs before dawn?

The door opened and Will came in with a large black duffel bag, dropped it, and started untying her wrists and feet.

She stayed silent, in total shock.

"I may regret this but you should come, in case we need you. Change and grab a jacket. The cliffs will be windy and cool."

"Thank you." Free, she hurried across the room to the bathroom, shut the door behind her, and dug through her bag. Judy had packed her dark jeans and pink T-shirt. It would have to do. She pulled the plum cardigan over her head and winced. Her ribs were still tender. Quickly, she moved her hair away for her face then slipped on her black flats. She freshened up and came out.

"Here." He pulled a black protective vest from his bag. "Put this over your sweater."

He tossed it to her, and she strapped it on.

Now their plan was in motion, fear engulfed her.

"Ready?" Will handed her a gun.

She held the heavy pistol and stared at it. Holy crap, she could die. Talking about facing off with Branson, piece of cake. Being near him again...yeah, she needed a moment to let it all sink in.

Will put his arm around her. "You don't have to do this."

She let out a long breath. "I can do this,

Branson's…"

"You're afraid of him and you should be."

"Could you at least sugarcoat it?"

"No." Will grabbed his black bag and opened the door. "After you."

When they'd searched the parking lot for the rental car he and Richard had and it wasn't there, Will handed her his bag and grinned. "Follow me." He picked a random sports car and smashed the window with a rock he lifted off the ground. Once he was in, he hotwired the ignition. She shook her head. He opened the door for her from inside. "Your chariot awaits."

She got in and they took off. The thin orange glow rose on the horizon. "Do you think we'll make it in time?"

"We should. Please follow my lead and stay behind me. And don't interfere with my angst toward my brother."

She had her own angst with Richard. "Fine. You stay alive."

"Worried about me, Kate?"

"No." She thought on her conversation with Richard mentioning the bloody mess at the Cliffs of Moher. "Maybe, a little. I want to see you eat your words about not getting married and working for your dad."

"He's not my dad."

"Then who is?"

"Don't know, doesn't matter. You really are too nosy."

"Since we're on the subject of me being nosy, are you sure Simon isn't your dad? I mean you and Richard and Jack, come to think of it, are all as perfectly chiseled as both of your parents."

"Then why am I the only one with dark hair?"

"My sister's blonde and both of my parents are brunettes. And Jack's hair is brown."

"I don't resemble Richard or Jack, and our sister, Charlotte, is blonde."

"Are you saying your mom had an affair?"

"Who knows? I'm not his son. Leave it alone."

She touched his arm. "I thought we were friends."

"We are."

"Then talk to me. You're upset, and I need a distraction."

"You won't stop pestering me until I tell you, will you?"

"True."

"I overheard a conversation between my parents when I turned nineteen. My mum said to Simon she wished I was his real son."

"When your nasty attitude started?"

He shrugged.

"Have you talked to them about it?"

"It's not exactly afternoon tea conversation."

"You make it afternoon tea conversation. They seem like good parents and I'd like to know more of the softer side of you."

"I don't have a softer side."

"Of course not. Besides, I have some friends I'd like to set you up with."

He scowled. "What is it about you and my mum feeling like you need to set me up? I can get a woman anytime I want, never been a problem. But Jack could use a date."

"Maybe it never being a problem is the problem, and I can see Ashlee wasn't just a 'woman' to you."

"Then you'll understand why I'm fine on my own."

"For now, and it's clear you haven't come to terms with losing her and maybe you never will, but I'm here if you ever want to talk about it."

"Talking about it only makes it worse."

When Will parked the car at the visitors' center at the cliffs, she blurted, "I'm scared."

231

Will turned to her and squeezed her hand. "Makes two of us."

She closed her eyes as if to erase it and make it all go away. "You don't look scared."

"Kate."

Her eyes met his.

"Sheridan is here. You really don't have to do this. Stay, it's all right."

"No, if I stay here, it won't be good for Jack. I can do this." She gave him a weak grin.

He sighed. "Nice try. You're rather a terrible liar, not to mention Richard will kill me if I show up with you. After all, you're supposed to be tied up and safe at the room. If it were Ashlee in your place, I wouldn't let her do this."

"Thank you, Will. I always wanted a big brother. I will do this, and if Ashlee were in my place, something tells me she would, too…with or without your approval."

Will groaned. "Right, then, let's get Jack."

Chapter Twenty-Six
Revenge

The sun hadn't risen, so they used the black of night to shield themselves as they raced down the concrete steps of the visitors' center then on the grassy cliffs toward O'Brien's tower. Her legs moved even though they felt unsteady and weak.

"Stay behind me." Will crouched as they approached the stone building that resembled a small castle to her.

When they got to the door, it opened without warning. Richard came out, a furious scowl on his face.

Will gave him a left hook across his jaw, and the first round of the Bennett brothers boxing match started.

Russell came out to stand beside her. "Hope you don't have any hard feelings about being in lockdown."

He grinned over at her. "I should but find it hard to be upset with you."

"Glad to hear it. These two go at it often?" She searched for Sheridan.

"For years now. Sheridan, your stand-in, is on the roof. Warned us you were coming. She's the lookout for Branson and Jack."

When Richard's body slammed Will, she winced. "I really can't watch this. You want to stop it, or should I?"

Russell showed her his watch. "Give it thirty seconds. If not, I'll end it."

Will swept Richard's feet out from under him, and they both dropped on the floor coughing, bloody and battered.

She stood over them and frowned. "Feel better?" She glared at Richard.

They both stood, and the woman who had to be

Sheridan came down the stairs. "Sun's up and a helicopter landed on the cliffs. Showtime."

"Nice to see you, Sheridan. Thank you for assisting me once again." Will wiped the blood from his lip.

She gave him a firm nod. "We'll get him this time."

Will gave her a weak smile. "Let's head out to Branson. You two can wait in here." He followed Sheridan outside.

Kate and Richard faced one another.

"How and why did you come?" He squinted. His right eye was already bruising.

"Will had a pocket knife and you shouldn't make choices for anyone but yourself."

He pulled her into his arms and kissed her. "I'm very upset with you right now."

"I'm more upset with you." She cradled his face in her hands and kissed him. "As soon as this is over, I'm locking you in Russell's cell but not before I tie you up."

He grinned. "Can't wait."

She pulled out a gun from her jacket.

"What are you doing?"

"I'm not actually going to listen to Will. We should keep watch and make sure things go down smooth."

He laughed. "You are brave. You do realize there's a sociopathic killer out there? I can do the watching, you stay put."

"I'm not listening to you, either." She followed him out the door, and they crouched down and peered around the archway to the wide concrete steps and path along the edge of the cliff.

The helicopter was in the grass behind the tower.

"Where are they?" he whispered.

She searched the area and heard voices. "To the right of us I think."

They moved low and around the right of the tower to Branson with Jack and three men on the top steps.

Will, Sheridan, and Russell were in front of them.

Will threw down a grey briefcase and nodded to Jack. "It's all there. You can let Jack go." He put his arm around Sheridan who kept her head down.

Branson tightened his grasp on Jack's arm. She could see Jack begin to sway and he shivered when the wind picked up.

She gripped his arm. "He's in bad shape."

Branson laughed. "I'll have my men count the money, but I'm going to have to kill Jack." He threw Jack to the ground and kicked him with the steel tip of his boot. "She's not Kate."

A woman of action, she knew she had to show herself to stop Jack's execution.

She plowed forward to run out, but Richard reached for her, slowing her momentum. His attempted grip brushed across her arm without a tight hold, freeing her to sprint over to Jack. All guns were drawn and pointed at opposing targets.

"No! I'm here, let him go."

Around her, everything happened faster than light and yet strangely in slow motion.

Shouting.

The metallic ping of bullets flying through the air.

Blam! Blam! Richard shooting two of Branson's thugs in the head. The pair dropping like flies.

Branson grabbed Kate and yanked her to his side, his gun jammed to her throat.

Branson's lone surviving man fled to the helicopter with Sheridan on his heels. Russell lifted Jack to his feet and started toward the parking lot.

She trembled, Branson's touch invoking horrible memories. He dragged her down the tower's concrete steps and over the small stone wall toward the cliff's edge. Will and Richard stalked toward them, guns aimed.

Branson pointed his gun at Richard then Will.

"Stop or I'll push her over!" He nudged her closer to the edge.

"This is between us, Branson. Let her go and we'll have it out, man-to-man, no weapons." Will tossed his gun over the cliff.

What? Why didn't he keep the gun! She gave Will a look of disapproval.

Branson jerked Kate around to face Richard—who already aimed at Branson's forehead, his finger on the trigger.

"I'll decline your offer and put a bullet where it will do the most damage. Since you didn't get to see me kill your wife, I think you should watch this." Branson glared into her eyes. "Nothing personal, darlin—"

Will lunged at him.

Kate was knocked aside. Off-balance, she fell, hitting and tumbling across the ground.

Richard rushed to her. The tender words he spoke came out muffled combined with the sea birds' faint cries. The united noises echoed with the wail of the waves crashing against the cliff barricades below.

The stinging pain all through her, bone chilling. The crisp air high on top of the precipice edge mingled with the agony and numbed her senses.

"Thank God." His voice remained muffled, but the noises had separated enough she could just make out the words. "The vest saved you, but the bullet grazed your side."

Movement in her peripheral caught her attention, and she turned her head. Behind him, Will and Branson warred for the pistol.

"Go!" She sat up.

In a flash, he scooped her up, depositing her behind the small stone wall. With her behind the protective barricade, he sprinted toward the fight.

She dared to peek over the wall. The nightmare beyond unfolding.

Will stumbled and flinched—bullets from Branson's gun slamming into him.

With a cry of shock and rage, Richard shot Branson repeatedly until his magazine depleted.

On wobbly legs, she clambered over the low stone barrier. Branson's body shuddered before falling still. Richard kicked the gun out of the dead man's grip.

Not far away, Will lay on the ground, already pale, a dark-red patch spreading rapidly across his shirt.

"No, no, no..." Violently shaking, she somehow made it to Will and Richard.

"Let's get you inside, mate." He had his arm firmly around his brother.

Will made a weak attempt to push him away. "Go to hell." His voice was more a whisper than a roar.

Chapter Twenty-Seven
Take It Easy

"If you come along." They stumbled in the tower door.

"You shouldn't have given me your vest," she mumbled before her voice broke.

Will let out a weak laugh then dropped to the floor. "I'm dying...and you're scold-ding me."

His complexion was ghost white. "Don't tell Richard what I told you about hearing my parents," he whispered in her ear. Turning his head to his side, he coughed up blood.

"Don't start." She tore off the vest he should have been wearing then pulled her sweater off and under his head. "You're going to be okay. Richard will see to it." She hoped but then lost it when Richard's devastated eyes met hers.

"I have to stop the bleeding, Will." He covered him with his jacket.

"Always the optimist." He gave him a weak grin. "You did good, little brother."

She bit her lip.

"Don't cry, but y-you can kiss m-me...if you want." Will gripped her hand.

He was comforting her on his death bed. It made her cry even harder.

"You already got your kiss."

Will fisted Richard's shirt. "My baby, please, Richard, go to Madelyn. Russell knows where she is."

Richard cleared his throat. "No, you'll go to her soon enough, mate. I just have to get you in hospital."

"Branson's dead, everyone's safe. Richard," he groaned. "You're Madelyn's guardian. Change Ashlee's tombstone. It's all in order. I want to be buried beside my wife."

"Won't be necessary."

"It's alright, mate, let me be... Marry me, Kate." Will grinned.

She laughed through tears. "First thing we'll do when you're better."

"You only agreed because I'm dying." His breathing slowed, and he moaned. "You promised," he whispered to her before the last breath left his body.

Richard shook his head and kept tending to Will's mortal wounds. He smeared the tears over his cheeks with the heel of his hand.

"Richard, he's gone."

***

The chill of death left Will's body, and a warm light moved through him. His spirit stood next to his lifeless remains.

"You stubborn man."

He turned around to see Ashlee behind him.

She embraced him, and he fell into the arms of the only woman he'd ever loved.

"I tried so hard to keep you from dying." She touched his cheek.

"And I've thought of nothing else. I've missed you, Mrs. Bennett." He tilted her chin up.

"What about Maddie?"

"You and I both know I couldn't have done it without you. I would have loved her, yes, but part of me left with you." He glanced over to Richard and Kate, still taking in what had happened. "They'll do a fine job. Maddie will be better off with two parents."

He kissed her and smiled. "Being with you is the only thing I've ever been good at."

She grinned. "Not true, but I love you, too. Let's go, but first you should say goodbye."

"Can they see us?"

"Not yet. I shouldn't do this, but I want them to know you're okay and to remember why they know each other so well." Ashlee smiled up at him.

"How do they know each other so well?"

"The accident. You should remember the Hereafter now, too."

"Right, I thought she was you but wondered why you were wearing such a showy dress."

"Ready for them to see us?" Ashlee squeezed him, still in his arms.

"As I'll ever be."

***

Richard tended to Will, still trying to bring him to life.

"Take it easy," Will said.

When Richard and Kate saw his spirit standing beside Ashlee's, they stood.

Kate stared, dismayed with grief and delight, a strange combination.

Will grinned at Richard. "Madelyn's yours now. Please tell her about us."

Richard wiped his eyes. "Every day."

"You'll remember the Hereafter but I'm not sure how long it will last," Ashlee said to them. "Your memory will be only you two were in the accident and met on the beach."

He gripped her hand, and they exchanged knowing glances of their time in waiting.

"And thank you, Richard, for *trying* to stop Will." Ashlee wrapped her arms around her husband.

"It was you, Kate, in the Hereafter." Will made eye contact with her. "You were wearing sunglasses, which is why I mistook you for Ashlee. Why the flashy dress?"

She grinned shakily. "A bridesmaid."

Will frowned. "Must have been some wedding."

"The worst."

"It's time." Ashlee gave Will a sad stare.

He moved in front of Richard. "I'm proud of you, everything you've done and become." Will nodded to him in approval.

"Figures it took you dying to tell me."

"Better late than never. Goodbye, Brother."

Ashlee and Will walked out the door and into the sunrise before they disappeared.

"I don't like watching people vanish. I hated the way you vanished." She remembered their interrupted kiss in the Hereafter.

"Dreadful to say the least." His jaw flexed. "You didn't listen to me after all, did things your way and didn't wait for me to come to you in New York."

"Once Judy had the idea in my head, I had to come to England, deep down I guess I knew I'd find you."

He embraced her. "Would you come with me, to tell my parents about Will and see Madelyn? I don't want to be away from you."

"I'm not letting you out of my sight."

He kissed her then they stood in each other's arms for a long while before Richard carried Will's body away from the cliffs.

***

"Hope I've cured your meddling ways, lass," Henry said to Charlotte on their walk to meet Will and Ashlee.

"My meddling ways didn't deserve the scare you gave me at your little white lie."

"It was necessary to stop you from putting your nose where it doesn't belong."

"I knew it didn't make sense; all of my brothers

dying. But to your great relief, I'm out of the meddling business for a while."

"Why?" Henry grinned at her.

"I have a new potential job, thanks to Perry." She smiled. "I'm up ten spots on the angel list for good behavior."

Henry shook his head. "Heaven help us all."

Chapter Twenty-Eight
Here, There, and Everywhere

The day had been the weepiest of her life. Watching Richard tell his parents what had happened had drained every tear she'd ever held onto. And he had been straightforward with the police about Will's revenge for Branson. The police had some questions for Russell and Jack, but Sheridan had left before they came. Richard's being a pillar of strength throughout the day impressed her. Not only had they gone to the hospital where Jack would be for a few days, but he handled everything. Even called the O'Keefes and told them what had happened and he'd be coming for Madelyn.

She waited for him now at the Bennett Hotel in Dublin. They were in his family's penthouse. He had stepped in the hall to talk to the hotel manager who had brought them some clothes. They needed something to wear other than attire covered in blood. She tightened her robe and combed out her wet hair while she gazed over the city of Dublin from the large window. The elegant room dimly lit by a few lamps.

He walked in and gave her a weak smile before wandering to the shower shell-shocked.

Her zombie state had her longing for sleep but her mind set on relief at having their mystery déjà vu solved. The Hereafter seemed like a dream, but she knew it had been all too real.

He came up behind her in loose-fitting jeans and held her in his arms. She leaned against him, the urge to cry overwhelming.

Turning to face him, she rested her head against his bare chest. "I can't stop." She sniffled. "When I think I'm done, I start all over again."

"I'm having the opposite problem. I'm still in

shock, can't really believe it yet. How's your side?" He pulled away from her and stared into her eyes. He'd cleaned the flesh wound at the hospital when they checked in on Jack.

"Better." She reached up with care and touched his black eye, heavyhearted it had resulted from the scuffle with Will.

He tightened his jaw.

"I know there's nothing I can say or do to make you feel better, Dr. Bennett, but I'm here."

"You're wrong, Ms. Adams." He cupped her face and kissed her. "You can help me forget. For tonight, nothing else matters but you."

"And after tonight?" She stared, lost in his eyes as he untied her robe and it slid down her shoulders.

"Only you, forever." He enveloped her in his arms.

***

Did it always rain at funerals? She stood beside Richard who held a sleeping Madelyn in his arms and an umbrella over their heads. It had poured the day they buried her dad, and the steady drizzle around them didn't seem to want to let up.

Once they could muster the energy to leave the hotel room after a long and perfect night, he wanted to get to Madelyn immediately. By midmorning, they were on the road to Shannon and at the O'Keefes where they met his adorable niece.

Seeing Will and Ashlee had helped them both deal with his death, but it still hurt. And to both their surprise, they both still remembered the Hereafter. He had followed Will's last wishes like he promised. He'd be buried beside Ashlee whose tombstone read Anna Fitzpatrick. The O'Keefes explained he and Ashlee went by Dylan and Anna Fitzpatrick as they were hiding from Branson. Her tombstone would be replaced with her real name as soon as possible.

She glanced over at Jack on the other side of her. Bad shape put mildly, his thrashed appearance and stoic stare revealed his recovery would be a long one. His broken arm in a cast, Jack wrapped the other one around his mom.

Veronica barely stood for five minutes before bending over, shoulders shaking with each sob that escaped her. She could only imagine the grief she carried. Simon came across no better.

She wiped her eyes for the umpteenth time. She'd cried enough the past week to go her whole life without ever needing to shed another tear.

When the service was over, Richard turned to her. "I should stay with my parents. Would you mind taking Maddie to the O'Keefes?"

"Happy to." She lifted the sleeping baby in her arms.

He walked them to the car and kissed her cheek. "It may be after dark before I return."

"We'll be fine." She carefully placed Madelyn in her car seat then followed the O'Keefes to their B&B.

The O'Keefes went to their room to rest. She went to put Maddie, still asleep, in her crib but decided to hold her in her arms and sit in the rocker instead. She covered her up with a soft lavender blanket and stared at her while she slept. She loved her already, even though she'd only known her days.

And when Maddie was awake, seeing Will's eyes stare at her proved both heartbreaking and amusing. Definitely a perfect mix of her parents. She kissed her forehead and held her closer when she started to smile in her sleep. How could she ever leave Madelyn or Richard? Her heart belonged to both of them, so she would stay and make a new life. She and Judy would open up the dance studio and she'd still do what she loved.

She went over to the crib and carefully put Maddie down. Time to call Judy and tell her she would be her partner in the dance studio.

And she'd have a better life than she ever imagined, if Richard would agree to marry her.

She quietly exited the room after smiling at the sleeping baby she hoped would belong to her soon.

***

"Miss me?" Richard asked.

She yawned and clasped his offered hand.

She stood up from the couch in the sitting room. She'd waited up as long as she could. "Your parents?"

He shook his head. "Misery doesn't quite describe it. And it brings memories of Charlotte's death. How was Maddie?"

"Fun and messy. I gave her a bath and put her to bed. The O'Keefes went to the neighbors to play cards."

Richard put his arm around Kate when the O'Keefes walked in. "And right in time."

"Hurry on then, lad." Mrs. O'Keefe hugged Richard. "We'll be fine and tend to Maddie for the night."

"For the night? You just got here." She pouted at him.

"You and I have plans." He led her to the door.

"We do? Let me get my shoes, then." She stepped into her black heels and smoothed her hands down the front of the dress she still wore from the funeral.

Once outside in the cool night air, he draped his suit jacket over her shoulders then wrapped his arm around her.

"Where are we going?" she asked.

"Don't you like surprises, Ms. Adams?"

"No, 'man of every woman's dreams,' I don't."

He laughed. "Ah the memories of hearing your

thoughts. Quite relieved it's over."

They turned toward a two-story home with a small garden.

"Nerve-racking." When he moved his arm around her, she melted into him.

"Agreed." He stopped her at the front door.

"Who lives here?"

"Will and Ashlee did." He opened the door for her and stepped aside.

The roaring fireplace illuminated the charming living room and the cushions from the couch placed in a row in front of it.

He shut the door and walked up beside her.

"You haven't been with your parents this whole time, have you?"

He shook his head. "Shall we?" He motioned for her to sit in front of the fire.

She sighed. "If it were smaller in here, it would be like being in our little cottage."

He sat beside her. "I thought so. Do you like it?"

"I do. Will and Ashlee must have been happy here."

"The O'Keefes tell me they were. I think we should stay here awhile, let Maddie get more acquainted with us before we take her home."

"Home?"

"Yes, I have something to ask you, but first I need to apologize for drugging you and leaving you tied up with Will. There's an apology you don't hear every day."

She couldn't stop smiling. "Unexpected, but I know why you did it and forgive you."

"Good." He tucked her hair behind her ear. "I know things have been hectic and gloomy with the funeral and all, but being with you somehow makes it bearable."

She hugged him. "What can I do? I feel like I

haven't done much."

He rested his chin on her head. "Stay with me."

"Done."

"Forever."

She opened her mouth, but nothing sprang from her lips.

"I know you had plans and our accident changed them. And I know we've hardly had time to go out and get to know the little things about each other. I don't know your middle name, favorite color, or favorite music yet. But I do know I loved you when I saw you in the god-awful dress."

She wiped the tears from her eyes.

"And I see I've made you cry again. I really should learn to write a good poem."

"Have something in my eye is all, go on."

"Right, then. I loved you, but I fell in love with you every moment after."

"I loved it the first time you told me, but nothing beats you saying it now," she whispered.

"Wasn't sure if you remembered because of how I disappeared shortly thereafter, glad you do. I'm limiting my time at the hospital. I'll only work enough to keep my license current. I know now I'm responsible for Madelyn it makes things—"

"Perfect." She smiled.

He kissed her gently. "Glad we agree. What I want more than anything is a long normal life with you. No guns or drugs involved...and to get to know Madelyn and hopefully have more children someday and for you to dance again. I realize I'm rambling, stop me anytime. What I'm trying to say is—"

"Wait." She brought her finger to his lips. "I have something I need to ask you."

He grinned. "It better be more important than what I was about to ask you."

"Marry me, and how old are you?"

"Thirty and you are direct."

"Life's too short not to be."

He nodded. "I agree and will marry you on one condition." He stood and then pulled her to her feet. He pulled a princess-cut diamond ring from his shirt pocket. "If you tell me how old you are." He got down on one knee. "You marry me."

She pulled him up. "Twenty-five and I asked you first."

He laughed. "I will. You'll marry me, then?"

"Yes."

He slipped the ring onto her finger, and she ogled the rock. *I'm engaged to Dr. Love!* She jumped into his arms.

He kissed her then stared into her eyes. "As I recall, you wished to be able to hear me play the guitar someday when we were in the Hereafter." He picked up the guitar from beside the fireplace and sat on the couch.

She dropped to the cushions in front of the fire.

When he played the first few chords to "Here, There and Everywhere," she bit her lip. "Now you've done it. I can't see. Whatever's in my eye has spread. We have a song."

He rested the guitar on the couch and moved to the floor with her. "Yes, we do." He tilted her chin up with his hand. "Keep your eyes on me, Ms. Adams. I'm not going anywhere."

Epilogue

Richard returned home from a late shift at the hospital and heard Madelyn talking. In her sleep again? A stream of light from the hall haloed her precious face.

He rubbed his hand over his eyes. "Who are you talking to, Maddie?"

She grinned. "Uncle Daddy!" She jumped out of bed and into his arms.

"Quiet, love. We don't want to wake Aunt Mum." He put her back into bed, and her wide smile had him suspicious and bewildered. What was she up to, and how could she be three years old already?

Richard sat down beside her. "How's the gum?"

"Good." Madelyn reached under her pillow and handed Richard a gumball.

Richard pointed to the door and grinned. "Aunt Mum still doesn't know about your bubble gum stash, then?"

"No way. Say hi to Daddy."

Richard popped the gum in his mouth and grinned. "Hello to Daddy." The thought of his dead brother coming to see Madelyn brought goose bumps popping on his arms.

Maddie grinned. "He says he's better looking."

Richard laughed and nearly choked on his gum. He glanced around the room. "You tell your daddy he has no manners."

She giggled. "Uncle Daddy, let's show him our big chew bubbles!"

Richard hushed her and nodded. "Fine, sweet girl, but keep it down. If Aunt Mum finds out we're having a bubble-gum-blowing contest in the middle of the night, we'll both be in a time-out for a while." He grinned.

"Me first." She chewed and brought a huge bubble to her lips then smacked it loud to pop it. The gum covered her nose and cheek.

"Better than last time. I think you've been practicing. Watch this." He blew a small bubble and let it deflate.

She shook her head. "You need more practice."

He laughed.

"My turn." She stood on her bed.

"This will be the last one, Madelyn. I have to get to bed." He kissed her cheek. "All right, go for it."

"Watch, Daddy." Madelyn grinned over at the window and blew an even bigger bubble than before. But this time when it popped, part of it went into her long, dark curls.

He moved to get the gum out of her hair, but she gripped it before he did and squeezed it into more hair.

The bedroom light came on, and he jumped up and swallowed his gum.

"What's going on?" Smiling, Kate walked to Maddie and lifted her in her arms. "What's this?"

"We showed Daddy how big my chew bubbles get."

Kate peered around the room. "Daddy?" She glanced at him.

"He came to see me." Maddie yawned.

"How nice, Daddy's seen your big chew bubbles, so we can head to the kitchen for some peanut butter so we don't have to cut off your pretty curls."

Maddie shook her head. "But I have to say bye."

Kate put her down, and she ran over to her window.

"Bye, Daddy!" After hugging the air, she ran over to Kate.

"Please get the rest of the gum from under Maddie's pillow so this doesn't happen again." She winked, kissing his cheek before walking out to the kitchen with Maddie.

"Right." He lifted the pillow and snatched the three pieces of gum.

They brought Madelyn to her bed, and though she'd fallen asleep in Aunt Mum's arms, they still wanted to cherish one last moment with this sweet, precocious child.

Kate gently tucked her in then stood next to him as they watched her sleep. "Do you think Will came here?" she whispered to him.

He laid his hand on her growing belly. "No doubt. Madelyn said he mentioned he was better looking."

She swallowed her laugh. "Let's get to bed, ugly duckling."

When he tickled her and chased her out the door, she screamed.

Made in the USA
Columbia, SC
11 October 2020